# wondergirls

# Troublemaker

## Jillian Brooks

SCHOLASTIC INC.
New York  Toronto  London  Auckland  Sydney
Mexico City  New Delhi  Hong Kong  Buenos Aires

ISBN 0-439-35491-9

Copyright © 2002 17th Street Productions,
an Alloy, Inc. company
All rights reserved.
Published by Scholastic Inc.

 Produced by 17th Street Productions,
an Alloy, Inc. company
151 West 26th Street
New York, NY 10001

SCHOLASTIC and associated logos are trademarks and/or registered trademarks of Scholastic Inc.

12 11 10 9 8 7 6 5 4 3 2 1     2 3 4 5 6 7/0

Printed in the U.S.A.          01
First Scholastic printing, May 2002

# chapter
## ONE

Dear Diary,

This is going to be an awesome year! I was really nervous about starting middle school, but everything's gone great so far. First my old summer-vacation pal Traci McClintic moved here to Wonder Lake, giving me one instant friend. Then Arielle Davis and Amanda Kepner actually decided they wanted to hang out with me—boring, shy, quiet Felicia Fiol.

It's still kind of hard to believe. Amanda's great, but I don't think she ever even noticed me back in elementary school. And Arielle . . . well, she's just about the coolest and most popular girl in Wonder Lake. I'm still not sure why she wants to hang out with me, but hey, I'm not complaining!

"Watch it, Felicia!" Traci yelled. "Quentin's making a break for it!"

I lunged after the little brown dog that was heading for the thick glass doors that led into Wonder Lake Hospital. Traci, Amanda, Arielle, and I were trying to load a bunch of animals from my dad's shelter back into the van. We had just finished another successful visit from Healing Paws, the pet therapy program that my friends and I created. "Get back here, Quentin," I told the little dog, trying to sound stern.

It wasn't easy. Quentin—this adorable little mixed-breed dog—stopped when I reached him and sat up on his hind legs, wagging his stumpy tail and panting at me eagerly.

"Okay, you've got to admit that's cute," Amanda said, nudging Arielle in the ribs.

Arielle rolled her eyes. "Whatever," she said. But she couldn't help smiling.

I scooped up Quentin and headed toward my dad's ancient blue van, which was parked near the curb outside the hospital entrance. Dad was leaning in through the rear doors, arranging the dog crates that were stacked back there.

"I guess Quentin really likes being a therapy dog," Traci said as she followed, leading a chubby black Labrador. "He wants to go back in and entertain some more patients."

"Put Quentin in the blue crate, Felicia," my dad said. "Traci can put Blackie there in the big one, and we'll be all set."

I shoved a wriggly Quentin into the crate my dad pointed out, but the small dog immediately moved to shoot back out again. I managed to shut the metal door just in time. Then I stepped back to give Traci room.

"Thanks for driving us again, Mr. Fiol," Traci said cheerfully as she unclipped the Lab's leash and pushed him gently into his crate.

"I'm happy to do it," Dad replied with a smile. "Pet therapy is a really worthwhile cause. Besides that, it's good publicity for the shelter. The more people see how nice our animals are, the more likely they'll be to adopt one from us."

It was just like Dad to think about something like that. The Wonder Lake Animal Shelter is his life. He started it a couple of years ago, and he works really hard taking care of the animals and finding them good homes.

My friends love coming to the shelter, especially Traci and Amanda. Both of them are almost as crazy about animals as my dad. They come over all the time to help him clean out the pens and runs in the shelter building behind our house and feed all the animals that live there. Arielle usually tags along with them, even though she's not really as into animals or, more important, getting dirty. Having an excuse to hang out with the three of them almost makes it worth the fact that I spend all my spare time cleaning up dog doo and trimming cats' claws. Well, all my time during the week, that is. On weekends, I live at my mom's apartment over the bakery she runs in town. She and Dad got divorced about two years ago.

"Okay, everybody back here's ready to go," Traci said, stepping back from the Lab's crate.

"Great," Dad said. "Let's hit the road, girls."

Soon we were all taking our places in the lumpy seats in the van. It was Traci's turn to ride in the front, so I ended up squished into the long backseat with Amanda and Arielle. I didn't mind, though. It was still kind of hard to believe sometimes that I was actually *friends* with those two. Last year, back in our elementary school math class, I spent way too much time staring at the backs of their heads and wondering what it would be like to be their friend. And now here I was, hanging out with them almost every day. It was like a dream come true, though I would never admit it out loud. It would sound way too dorky.

Dad started the engine and pulled out of the hospital's parking lot. Soon we were turning onto Wonder Lake's main street, passing the town green, which is surrounded by a bunch of stores and other buildings. My house is on the outskirts of town, on the opposite side from the hospital.

"I still think we should have brought that cute black-and-white rabbit," Arielle commented as we drove past the town hall and the post office.

Amanda tossed her long, straight brown hair

over her shoulder and glanced at Arielle. "Why don't you say that a few dozen more times?" she said. "I don't think every person in Wonder Lake has heard it yet."

I turned away from the van window and giggled nervously. Amanda and Arielle have been friends forever—they're almost more like sisters than regular friends. Unfortunately, that means they argue a lot. They hardly ever stay mad at each other for more than about thirty seconds, but it still makes me a little nervous. Especially after the big fight all four of us had at the beginning of the school year.

"I just think it's kind of boring to bring *only* dogs, that's all," Arielle said. "That's not pet therapy, it's *dog* therapy. Besides, that rabbit is adorable—he smells a lot better than those dogs, too."

At that moment, Quentin let out a sharp, annoyed bark. That made all of us laugh.

Traci twisted around in her seat to look back at us. "I think Quentin said he smells a lot better than your new peach perfume, Arielle," she quipped.

Amanda and I laughed, but Arielle looked kind of annoyed. She and Traci didn't exactly hit it off when Traci first moved to town, and they still manage to rub each other the wrong way sometimes. That was sort of what started that big fight we had.

I decided it was time to distract them before they started sniping at each other. "Um, the dogs-only thing was sort of my fault," I admitted. "I helped Dad decide which animals to bring, and I thought since it was only our second visit, we shouldn't take too many. Maybe we can take the rabbit next time."

"That's a good idea, Felicia," Dad spoke up as he eased the van to a stop at a stop sign and looked both ways. "Rabbits and cats can be wonderful therapy animals if they have the right temperament, like that black-and-white bunny. And they're perfect for people who are afraid of dogs."

"How could anyone be afraid of dogs?" Traci said wistfully as the van rumbled on through the intersection.

I could guess what Traci was thinking. She was dying for a dog of her own. Unfortunately, her older brother, Dave, is totally allergic to all kinds of fur. He practically breaks out in hives if he sees a cat or dog on TV.

Amanda, Arielle, Traci, and Dad started chatting about the patients we'd visited that day. I sat back and listened for a while, thinking for the hundredth time how nice it was to have best friends. It seemed too good to be true sometimes. At my old school, everyone thought I was such a brain, no one wanted to hang around with me. I got used to being alone. I still worried that the others were going to figure out that I wasn't cool or interesting enough to be friends with them after all. Then I would have to go back to hanging out with my usual group—me, myself, and I.

I shuddered and tuned back in to the conversation. Arielle was checking her watch.

"I can't believe the weekend's almost over," she said with a sigh.

"Don't remind me," Traci put in. "I have a bunch of word problems to do for math class tomorrow. And I still need to torture myself with my clarinet."

I shot her a sympathetic look. "Are you still worried about that new piece we're learning in orchestra?"

"Sure, aren't you?" Traci rolled her eyes and sighed. "I can't believe Mom picked it out. Who does she think we are, the Chicago Philharmonic or something?"

I nodded. The flute part for the new piece was pretty tough. I'd been practicing it as much as possible since we got the music last week, and I still kept messing up a few tricky places. And the clarinet part looked even harder.

It probably didn't help Traci that her mother was Wonder Lake Middle School's new music teacher. Ms. McClintic teaches all the music classes, directs the marching band, and leads the orchestra. She also happens to be Traci's homeroom teacher this year. That had to be tough. I mean, Ms. McClintic is great. But it must be really weird to have your mother for a teacher.

Amanda checked her watch, too. "I hope Penny isn't waiting for me," she said. "I told her we'd be back by four."

Dad glanced at her in the rearview mirror. By this time, we were almost at the town limits. Soon we were bumping along on the country road that led to our house. "Don't worry," he said. "It's only five after four now. And we'll be home in about two minutes."

"Besides, it's not like Penny is ever on time for anything," Arielle put in.

"Who's Penny?" Traci asked Amanda. "Is that your stepmom's name?"

I was glad she'd asked, because I was wondering the same thing. But I also kind of felt like I should know already. It was a familiar feeling. Amanda and Arielle had been friends for so long that they knew everything about each other. And Traci was so friendly and outgoing that she was never afraid to ask questions if she didn't know something. That was one of the things I liked about her when we first met during summer vacation a few years ago. So that left me— always playing catch-up.

Amanda shook her head. "Penny Zinsser. She's an artist who lives down the street from me," she explained. "She's been my baby-sitter ever since I was little. She taught me everything I know about art." She frowned at Arielle. "And she's almost always on time."

Arielle just shrugged. For some reason, she looked kind of annoyed. "Whatever," she muttered.

Dad looked back at Amanda again. "I had a chance to speak to Penny when she came to pick you up the other day. Her art sounds really interesting."

"Uh-huh, it is." Amanda brushed a clump of dog hair off her flared jeans. "Penny is really cool, and she's an amazing artist—she paints and takes photos and stuff. But her main thing is these papier-mâché sculptures she makes. She has this huge pink moose in her dining room and a whole flock of penguins in the den. She even did a sculpture of me once. I don't know if you guys noticed it when you were over—it's in the dining room at my house."

"I don't think I've seen it," I said. Since Amanda and I had only been hanging out for a few weeks, I had been at her house just once.

"Me, neither," Traci put in. "I'd love to see it sometime."

Arielle rolled her eyes. "I've seen it, and trust me, you guys aren't missing much," she said. "It doesn't look anything like her."

Amanda frowned at her. "It's not supposed to be, like, an exact copy," she said, sounding miffed. "Penny's art is very, um, interpretive."

"Whatever." Arielle sniffed. "I guess I'm not 'interpretive' enough, then, because I've never seen a pink moose. And I'm not sure I really want to."

Penny's art sounded a little weird to me, too. But it didn't surprise me that Amanda liked that kind of stuff. She has really interesting taste. You could tell that just by looking at her funky hippie-style jeans and gauzy embroidered blouse. She gets most of her outfits at vintage clothing stores and flea markets. Her look is the total opposite of Arielle's sleek, modern style. Arielle always looks perfect from the top of her smooth auburn hair to her pink-painted toenails.

There was a moment of silence in the van. I wasn't sure why, but Arielle and Amanda seemed kind of annoyed with each other now. I looked around desperately, trying to think of a way to change the subject.

"Hey, you guys," I spoke up at last. "When's your next soccer game? Maybe Amanda and I could come and watch again."

Arielle looked happier right away. She loves soccer, and she's really good at it. Amanda likes to joke that playing soccer is the one thing Arielle does better than shopping. "We have a scrimmage on Friday," she said. "You could come watch that."

"You can watch, but I probably won't be playing," Traci muttered, staring out the window at the houses and trees along the side of the road. She was on the soccer team, too. "If I can't play that stupid new piece in orchestra, Mom will probably make me stay home and practice until I get it right."

Wow, Traci was more nervous about the orchestra piece than I'd realized. I kind of thought she was making too big a deal of it—the piece wasn't *that* hard. And Ms. McClintic really isn't very strict. But I didn't say anything. Traci has a pretty quick temper, and I could tell she was in no mood for criticism.

Dad glanced over at Traci. "I'm sure you'll get it, Traci," he said soothingly. "You're a terrific musician. Ryan told me you'll probably be first chair clarinet by next year."

Traci looked embarrassed. "What does *he* know?" she muttered. She glanced at my dad. "Um, I mean, thanks, Mr. Fiol."

Traci and Ryan Bradley don't really get along very well. Traci has a slight Southern drawl from living in South Carolina most of her life, and when she first came to Wonder Lake, Ryan made fun of how she talked all the time. Just about the only reason she talks to him at all is because he adopted this huge Saint Bernard puppy named Lola from the shelter recently. Lola's really cute. If it wasn't for Dave's allergies, I'm sure Traci would have adopted her herself.

Arielle grinned at me. "Hey, Felicia, didn't you say that Ryan was coming over to your house today?"

"Uh-huh," I said. "He and Lola are coming for

11

one of their free dog-training lessons." Dad offers free training to anyone who adopts a dog or puppy from the shelter. He thinks that informed pet owners are more likely to enjoy their pets and less likely to bring them back to a shelter if anything goes wrong.

"Hmmm," Arielle said. "It will be nice to see him. Won't it, Traci?"

Traci glanced back at her with a slight scowl. "Whatever floats your boat," she said curtly.

I wasn't sure why Arielle kept talking about Ryan, but I could tell it was getting on Traci's nerves. I tried to find a neutral topic, but my mind went blank. Nobody said anything for a long moment—except Quentin. He let out a few yips and then a howl.

"Sounds like Quentin can't wait to see Ryan, either," Arielle commented innocently.

Amanda glanced at her. "What's the deal?" she asked curiously. "Don't tell me you have the hots for Ryan Bradley, Arielle."

"No way." Arielle sniffed. "He's not *my* type."

Just then, Dad took the turn onto our long, steep driveway. A few seconds later, he was pulling to a stop in front of our white farmhouse.

"Here we are, girls," he said. "And look, we seem to have a welcoming committee."

I glanced out the window and saw a young-looking

woman I didn't recognize standing on the steps leading up to the screened-in porch. The woman was tall—almost as tall as my dad—with wavy, honey-colored hair pulled back in a long ponytail. She was wearing a bright blue dress with little multicolored birds printed all over it, dangly bead earrings, and moccasins.

Then Amanda leaned over me, rolled down the van window, and waved. "Hi, Penny," she called. "Sorry we're late."

Penny? I blinked, realizing this must be the artist baby-sitter Amanda had been talking about. She didn't look anything like I expected. Somehow I thought she'd be older, maybe with a sloppy gray bun. And a big smock stained with paint. Instead, she looked sort of like an adult, blond version of Amanda.

"It's okay, sweetie," Penny replied. "I just got here myself." Her voice was high and sort of lilting—almost like she was singing instead of speaking. She smiled as all of us climbed out of the van. "Hi, there, Arielle. How are you?"

"Fine," Arielle muttered. She didn't sound nearly as happy to see Penny as Penny sounded to see her.

Amanda gestured toward us. "Penny, these are my other friends—that's Traci McClintic, the one I was telling you about who just moved here from South Carolina."

"Oh, yes. You're from Charleston, right, Traci?" Penny said. "That's such a beautiful city."

"Hi," Traci said with a smile. "Yeah, it is great there. But it's pretty nice here, too." She pointed to a sparkly pendant at Penny's throat. "I like your necklace."

"Thanks!" Penny stroked the stone. "It's my very favorite crystal. I find it so centering—I almost never take it off."

Amanda nodded at me. "That's Felicia Fiol. Her mother runs that awesome bakery in town, and her dad runs the animal shelter here."

"Yes, we've met." Penny smiled at me for a second before turning to look at my dad. "Luis told me about his work when we met the other day. It sounds like he's doing a wonderful thing for this town. Wonder Lake has needed its own shelter for a long time."

Luis? I blinked. My dad is really nice and everything, but he can be sort of formal. Most people call him Mr. Fiol. Especially when they've just met him.

Dad's brown eyes crinkled a little at the corners when he smiled. "I'm just grateful that I can help," he said, passing one hand through his short, curly dark hair. "It's a tough job, but it's worthwhile."

Penny nodded. "Absolutely." She put her hand on Dad's arm briefly, then took it away.

I wrinkled my nose. Most people didn't pat Dad on the arm, either.

Amanda had made Penny sound like some kind of goddess or something. Now that I'd met her, she just seemed really ditzy.

Penny turned toward me. "Felicia, I was sorry I didn't get to meet you the other day when I came to get Amanda," she said. "Your dad gave me a little tour of the house, and I saw that adorable Eeyore night-light in your room. I wanted to tell you—I had one just like it when I was little!"

My jaw dropped. I could feel my cheeks going hot. Why hadn't I thrown that stupid night-light away by now? It wasn't like I really needed it anymore. In fact, I usually hid it whenever I knew my friends were coming over. I was too embarrassed to look at them, but I could hear Arielle start to giggle. I couldn't believe this. How could someone just blurt out a totally embarrassing story like that in front of everybody?

Worse yet, how could my own father show a complete stranger around my room without even checking with me first? And how could he stand there listening to her tell my friends all about it, smiling like nothing was wrong?

How was I ever going to live this down?

# chapter
## TWO

**Wonder Lake Animal Shelter Rules:**
1. *If you opened it, you close it—tightly.*
2. *Volunteers: Check list before feeding ANYTHING to the animals. Guests: Please don't feed the animals without permission.*
3. *Guests: Please don't try to pet the animals without permission. Our animals are usually friendly. But remember: If it has teeth, it can bite.*
4. *Veterinary emergencies: Call Dr. Jackson at 555-3489.*
5. *All adoptions require contract, home check, and references.*
6. *Free basic obedience training is available for your new pet. Ask Mr. Fiol for more information.*

I guess Traci noticed I wasn't too happy about Penny's little story because she cleared her throat and gestured toward the van. "Hey," she said. "We'd better get these guys out of their crates. I think Quentin has to take a leak." She hurried over and swung open the van's rear doors.

Penny blinked at her. "Quentin?" she repeated, sounding puzzled.

The latch on Quentin's crate must have been loose. When Penny said his name, he suddenly pushed his way right through the wire door. Hopping out of the back of the van, he raced up to us and barked.

Penny let out a loud gasp. "Wh-what's that dog doing here?"

She said the word *dog* in the same way someone might say *ax murderer*. Quentin just cocked his head, then trotted over to sniff at the hem of her skirt.

Penny jumped back and hid behind my father. She looked like she was shaking. What was her problem?

"What's the matter?" Dad asked, looking concerned.

"I—I don't do too well with dogs," Penny said in a frightened voice. "Actually, they terrify me. I was badly bitten by one as a child."

"Oops! Sorry, Penny. I forgot all about that." Amanda rushed forward and scooped up Quentin.

"Girls," Dad said. "Take that dog and put him away. Now."

I blinked. His voice was stern—like we'd done something wrong. But we hadn't.

"Okay," I said. "But Quentin didn't do anything wrong."

"Felicia, I said *now*." Dad frowned at me.

I couldn't believe he was making such a big deal out of this. With a shrug I headed for the shelter, carrying Lucy, a squirmy dachshund, and Edgar, a sleepy beagle mix.

Amanda followed, still holding Quentin. Glancing back, I saw my dad step forward to give the little dog a comforting pat as he passed. Then he put a hand on Penny's arm and hurried her toward the house as Traci reached into the van for the other dog.

"That was weird," Traci said when the four of us were inside the shelter building. "Your dad sounded kind of mad, Felicia."

I nodded. "Yeah." I thought it was weird, too. Why did Dad have to freak out like that in front of my friends? They already knew he was kind of stern, at least compared to a lot of other parents. But if he started acting so mean all the time, they might not want to come around anymore.

Amanda released Quentin into his pen. Then she straightened up and brushed back her hair. "He was just being polite," she said. "You know, to Penny. Because she was afraid."

"Yeah," Arielle murmured into my ear. "He must've realized what a loser Penny is."

I smiled. I couldn't help it. Maybe it wasn't nice, but Penny really did seem like a dweeb, no matter what Amanda said. That goofy crystal necklace.

Telling that dumb story about me. And what normal person could be afraid of a cute little dog like Quentin?

Amanda couldn't possibly have overheard what Arielle said—the animals were making too much noise. But she must have figured out it was something bad about Penny, because she frowned.

"Anyway, I'm just so glad you all finally got to meet Penny," Amanda said loudly. "She's really cool. And super-talented, too. Did I tell you she had her own show at the Wonder Lake Art Gallery last year? It got written up in the *Gazette* and everything."

"Really?" Traci sounded interested. "That's cool."

"Uh-huh." Amanda bent down to pat a calico cat who was sticking her paw out through the wire of her pen. "Her stuff is amazing."

Arielle rolled her eyes at me. "Come on, Felicia," she said. "It's getting a little stinky in here."

Maybe she was talking about the usual animal-shelter smells. Or maybe not.

I followed her outside. Behind us, I could hear Amanda and Traci chatting about Penny's art.

"Now Traci's in for it," Arielle muttered, glancing over her shoulder as we stopped near the water pump in the middle of the yard. "Once Amanda starts blabbing about how great Penny is, she never shuts up."

I laughed nervously. On the one hand, I was glad

I wasn't the only one who didn't think Penny was the greatest person in the world. On the other hand, I really, really, really hated it when my friends argued.

I glanced over my shoulder to make sure Amanda couldn't possibly hear us. "I know what you mean," I said. "Amanda seems to be crazy about her."

"Yeah." Arielle snorted. "Don't ask me why. Penny's a freak. She acts like she's Amanda's big sister or something instead of just her baby-sitter."

"Really?" I said. "That's weird."

I felt a little bit guilty for talking about Amanda behind her back. But it also felt kind of good to be gossiping with Arielle; it showed that she trusted me not to rat her out to Amanda. And that was a good thing. Wasn't it?

As Amanda and Traci emerged from the shelter, I looked around the corner of the house into the front yard. Dad and Penny were nowhere to be seen.

"Where did they go?" I asked.

"Maybe Penny's under the porch, hiding from a vicious toy poodle or something," Arielle suggested brightly.

Amanda glared at her. "Very funny," she said.

Arielle just shrugged.

"Could they be inside?" Traci asked. "Maybe Penny wanted a drink of water."

We headed up onto the screen porch and through the front door. "Dad?" I called. "Hello?"

There was no answer.

"Let's check the weed farm," I said.

The weed farm was what Dad and I called the overgrown area on the side of the house opposite the driveway. It must have been a nice flower garden a couple of owners ago, but now it was pretty much a mess. Dad also called it "the jungle."

We hurried back out to the yard. As soon as I opened the side door, I heard Penny's goofy, trilling laugh.

"There they are!" Amanda said.

I just stared. They were out there, all right, standing smack in the middle of the weed garden beside the cracked, old, cement birdbath.

And this time Dad had his *arm* around Penny's *shoulders!*

"Hey!" I called. My voice sounded kind of loud. I hurried through the door, almost tripping on the warped brick step. "What are you guys doing out here?"

Dad jumped a little. Was I crazy, or did he look sort of guilty?

"Oh, there you are, Felicia," he said. "I was just showing Penny around the yard while she waited for Amanda."

I felt my cheeks turning pink, even though I wasn't

exactly sure why. My dad was the one who should be embarrassed. Or maybe Penny. They were the ones acting weird, not me. Since when did Dad laugh and put his arm around some strange woman he'd just met? Especially a wacky, crystal-wearing, embarrassing-story-telling one like Penny? I was surprised the two of them even had anything to talk about. It was obvious that they didn't have a single thing in common.

"Well, Amanda's ready to go home now," I blurted. "And don't forget, Ryan's going to be here any minute for his *dog*-training lesson."

Penny flinched a little at the word *dog*. "Yes, Amanda and I had better be going," she said. "Sorry for barging in like this—I hope I didn't keep you from your work, Luis."

"No, no trouble at all," Dad said quickly. "It was really great seeing you again, Penny."

Was it my imagination, or was he blushing? It was hard to tell—he's pretty tan from being outside all the time with the animals. But his cheeks looked a little red.

Penny smiled at him. "Yes, this was lovely." Then she turned to me. "And it was so wonderful meeting you at last, Felicia," she gushed. "Amanda has told me so much about you."

"Okay," I muttered. "Um, I mean, thanks."

My friends and I followed as Dad and Penny

walked through the weeds toward the front of the house. Soon we were all standing in the driveway as Penny dug for her keys in her dress pocket.

"Well, bye," I said as soon as she found them. I was ready for her to be gone so my dad could start acting normal again.

"Thanks for the tour, Luis," Penny said.

"Anytime." Dad cleared his throat and stuck out his hand. He and Penny shook hands awkwardly. "Um, I'll call you. You know, with the name of that restaurant I mentioned."

"Okeydokey!" Penny said with a big smile.

Dad leaned over and opened the car door for her. Penny thanked him and slid inside. Amanda hurried around to the passenger side.

"Anyone want a ride home?" Amanda asked as she opened her own door.

"Sure! Is that okay?" Traci asked. She glanced through the open car window at Penny.

"Of course! The more the merrier," Penny told her with a smile.

"Cool! I'll be right back. I left my jacket inside." Traci dashed into the house.

"How about you, Arielle?" Penny asked. "Can we drop you off at your house?"

"No thanks," Arielle said stiffly. "My father is picking me up on his way home from playing golf."

Nobody said anything for a few seconds. Dad

cleared his throat a few times, and Penny kept on smiling her goofy smile. We all just stood around like that until Traci raced back toward us with her jacket flapping from her hand.

"Okay," she said breathlessly. "I'm ready. Thanks for waiting."

"No problem," Penny chirped. As Traci climbed into the backseat, Penny started the car and glanced at Arielle. "Sure you don't want to bum a ride with us?"

Arielle wrinkled her nose. "I told you," she muttered. "My dad's coming to get me."

She turned and walked away before anyone could say anything else. I followed her toward the house. Behind me, I heard the car turning around and moving down the driveway.

"Felicia!" Dad called.

I paused and turned around. "What?"

"I'm going out to the shelter," Dad said. "If Ryan comes to the house, just send him out, okeydokey?"

I blinked as he hurried off toward the corner of the house. Then I turned and walked slowly toward the porch steps. Arielle was standing there, waiting for me.

"That was weird," I said. "Dad doesn't usually use words like *okeydokey*."

Arielle snorted. "Penny's probably rubbing off on him."

"Yeah." I shuddered. "I wonder why she spent so much time hanging around here. I mean, she was just

25

supposed to pick up Amanda and leave, right? So what was with the tour and everything? She acted like she and my dad were new best friends or something. How weird is that?"

"Don't worry. Penny's like that with everyone." Arielle picked at a spot of peeling paint on the edge of the porch railing. "She's so friendly, it's ridiculous."

Normally, I didn't think being friendly was a bad thing at all. I wished I could act a little more outgoing myself sometimes.

But in Penny's case, Arielle was right. It *was* kind of ridiculous for Penny to act so friendly with my dad when they had nothing in common. It's not like they were ever going to be friends, or anything.

"So is your dad really supposed to pick you up on his way home?" I asked.

Arielle opened the door and headed across the screen porch. "He will be once I call and tell him to." She grinned.

When she called her father's golf club, he'd already left. But she was able to reach him on his cell phone. It turned out he was almost back to Wonder Lake.

"He'll be here in like two minutes," Arielle said as she hung up. She checked her watch. "Too bad. I guess I'll miss seeing the love of Traci's life."

"You mean Lola?" I said. Traci was crazy about

Ryan's big, goofy pup. I couldn't blame her. Lola was pretty cute, even if she did drool a little.

Before Arielle could answer, there was a beep from outside.

"Wow. That was fast." I glanced out the window and saw Arielle's father's black BMW pulling into the driveway.

"Walk me out, okay?" Arielle said.

"Sure."

We headed toward the front door. Before we reached it, there was another loud beep from the driveway, which started all the dogs barking. Arielle's father seemed a little impatient.

"See you tomorrow," Arielle called, grabbing her bag off the hall table and hurrying out the door.

I waved to her and wandered out to the backyard, thinking over the strange afternoon.

A few of the dogs were still barking out in the shelter. When I got a little closer, I heard another sound, too—either we'd gotten in some new parrots or something or Dad was whistling.

"Weird," I muttered. Dad wasn't usually the whistling type. What was with him today? I had no idea, but I knew I didn't like it.

"Yo! Incoming," a breathless voice called.

I turned and saw Ryan loping around the side of the house with Lola tugging and panting on the end of her leash. It was hard to tell if he was walking her or she was walking him.

"Hi," I greeted them both, bracing myself as Lola raced up to me. One of the things Dad and Ryan were working on was teaching her not to jump up on people. So far, she wasn't really getting it. She was a little too friendly for her own good sometimes.

"Sorry," Ryan said, dragging Lola back as the huge half-grown Saint Bernard put her paws on my chest and did her best to slurp my face off.

"No problem." I wiped my face on my arm and gave Lola a pat on the head.

She panted at me, drooling a little on my sneakers. Then she started snuffling around in the yard.

"Dad's in the shelter," I told Ryan.

"Okay, thanks," Ryan replied. But instead of heading for the building, he just stood there, looking around the yard.

I wasn't sure what else to say. I've known Ryan for a long time, but I wouldn't really call us close friends or anything. In fact, I wasn't sure I'd ever tried to have a conversation with him before, just the two of us.

"Um, have you practiced that new orchestra piece?" I blurted at last.

Ryan shrugged. "A little," he said.

I figured that meant "a lot." Ryan is really good at the violin, and he takes it pretty seriously. I think it's the *only* thing he takes seriously, actually.

I moved my feet as Lola wandered over and started drooling on my sneakers again. "Me, too," I said. "I need to practice more tonight, though. It's pretty hard. I'm a little worried about it."

"Yeah," he agreed. "But don't worry. You'll do fine." He cleared his throat and looked around some more. "So where's everybody else?" he asked. "I thought you guys were doing the pet therapy thing today."

"We are," I said. "I mean, we did. We just finished a little while ago, so the others went home." I wondered how he knew so much about our pet therapy schedule. Weird.

"Oh." Ryan bit his lip. Was it just me, or did he look a little bummed out?

For some reason, Amanda's earlier comment to Arielle popped into my head—*Don't tell me you have the hots for Ryan Bradley, Arielle.*

At the time, I'd just figured it was more of that best-friends-forever kind of teasing that those two always did. But what if it wasn't? What if Arielle really did like Ryan? And what if he liked her back? It would be really weird if they started dating. They seemed so different. But he seemed awfully disappointed to discover that I was the only one here. . . .

"Ryan!" Dad called, poking his head out of the shelter door. "There you are. I'll be with you in a

29

sec—I just need to finish feeding some puppies."

"That's okay," Ryan called back, already hurrying toward him. "I'll help you." He glanced at me over his shoulder. "See you."

"Bye," I responded, though he was already disappearing through the door with Lola at his heels.

I stared after him, wondering if my imagination was running away with me. Could Ryan really be interested in Arielle? They didn't exactly seem like the perfect couple. Arielle was probably the most popular girl in Wonder Lake's sixth grade—she always wore all the coolest fashions, was starting center on the soccer team, and knew absolutely everybody.

Ryan was pretty popular, too, but in a different way. He was always goofing off and cracking jokes, trying to entertain everyone. That made him fun to be around, but I wouldn't exactly call him cool. Or mature. Could Arielle possibly see something in him that I couldn't?

I sighed, my earlier good mood fading a little as I thought about that. People were so confusing sometimes. What did people who seemed to be so different see in each other? I know opposites are supposed to attract, but it just doesn't make much sense. Like take my dad and Penny . . .

My dad and Penny. I thought back to the little

scene in the weed garden. Even thinking about it still gave me a funny feeling in the pit of my stomach.

The way Dad put his arm around her shoulders. The way he smiled at her. How he said "okeydokey." The way he was whistling in the shelter.

I really don't understand people at all sometimes.

# chapter
## THREE

---

**sockrgrl0:** Hi Felicia! RU there? ORCHESTRA IS THE PITS!!!

**FiFiol:** Don't worry. U'll get it if u practice.

**sockrgrl0:** Ugh! U sound like my mom.

**FiFiol:** Sorry! :-)

**sockrgrl0:** It's ok. So whatz new with u? It was fun meeting Penny 2day, huh?

**FiFiol:** I guess.

**sockrgrl0:** She's really cool. On the way home we cranked up the radio & all 3 of us sang along in the car. It was fun. I can see y A likes her so much, u know?

**FiFiol:** I have 2 go. CU in school 2morrow, ok?

---

"Did you give that new cat his antibiotics this morning, Felicia?" Dad asked.

I yawned and checked my watch. The school bus would be arriving in a few minutes.

"Uh-huh," I replied. "I even got it all in him this time instead of all over my hands like yesterday."

Dad chuckled. "Thanks. I know he's not an easy

patient." He stepped over to scratch the cat in question, who was rubbing against the bars of his pen. "It'll all be worth it when that nasty puncture wound clears up, buster," he told the cat fondly. The cat meowed in agreement.

Moving a little farther down the row of cages, I gave some food to a couple of Lab mixes. I yawned again. I'd stayed up later than usual practicing the new orchestra piece. I had most of it down pretty well. But Traci was right that it was hard—I still wasn't too sure I'd be able to keep up with the rest of the orchestra at practice that afternoon.

I checked my watch again. The shelter was getting busier all the time. Almost every cage was full. I hoped that lots of these animals would be adopted soon. Usually I didn't help with morning feeding, but I knew Dad was really swamped this week, so I was doing what I could to help out.

We'd already fed about three-fourths of the animals, so it was a little quieter than usual. Most of the dogs and cats had their faces buried in their bowls, and the chickens in the large bird pen were pecking at their feed. The rabbits and ferrets hadn't been fed yet, but they didn't make much noise.

"It was nice meeting Penny yesterday, wasn't it?" Dad suddenly asked me.

I froze in the middle of refastening the latch to one of the ferrets' cages. "Penny?" I said.

"Yes." Dad smiled as he bent down to retrieve a cat's water dish. "She's quite an interesting person."

"I guess you could put it that way," I muttered.

Why was Dad still talking about Penny? I just didn't get it. First Amanda and now Dad—they seemed to think she was totally fascinating. Why? As far as I could tell, she was just a wacky, crystal-wearing, dog-fearing, too friendly, too talkative woman who made big sculptures of multicolored animals for a living. In other words, someone who had absolutely nothing in common with most *normal* people—especially my strict, old-fashioned, hardworking, dog-loving father.

We worked in silence for a moment. I wanted to ask Dad what was so interesting about Penny, but I didn't have the guts. Instead, I hoped that he would drop the whole topic and never mention her again.

Finally, Dad cleared his throat. "I think Penny enjoyed meeting you, too," he said. "She said some nice things about you when I was showing her around the yard."

"Really? That's weird," I said. "I mean, she only met me for like a split second. It's not like she knows anything about me."

"I suppose that's true," Dad agreed. "But she got a good first impression. And of course, she got to hear me bragging about what a great kid you are."

"No kidding," I muttered, thinking of that embarrassing night-light story. Was that what Dad considered bragging?

Dad took a deep breath and glanced at me. "Anyway," he said, "I, uh, was thinking. That is, I was considering calling Penny sometime. To see if she wants to get together again."

For a second, I thought he meant all of us. Ugh.

Then I realized he meant just the two of them— him and Penny. Like, on a date. I gulped.

But why? What in the world would they find to talk about on a date? Their work? As far as I knew, Dad didn't know anything about papier-mâché art. And Penny couldn't even hear the word *dog* without ducking for cover. Their families? Not only did Penny not have any kids, but she didn't even know enough to realize that she shouldn't go blabbing about nightlights in front of people's friends.

Dad was still looking at me. "Well?" he asked expectantly. "What do you think?"

I hesitated. I knew what I wanted to say, if only I had the guts: Bad idea, Dad. You two have absolutely nothing in common. She's annoying. You can do better.

But I couldn't say that. I knew it wasn't really fair, and Dad seemed so excited. There was no way I could just come right out and tell him what I really thought of Penny.

Still, maybe there was another way. . . .

"Um, I thought what she said about that crystal she was wearing was really interesting," I said, trying to sound sincere. "Do you really think a piece of rock can be 'centering' like she said?"

Dad blinked. "Oh," he said blankly. "Well, I don't know—I suppose it's best to keep an open mind about such things. I'm sure she'd explain it to you if you asked."

As if. I didn't especially want to have any kind of conversation with Penny, let alone a discussion of crystal power. And I couldn't imagine my dad did, either.

I decided to switch to another angle. "It's too bad she's so afraid of dogs," I commented casually. "I guess that means she won't be hanging around here too much, huh? I mean, we've practically got dogs coming out of our ears." I gestured to the row of kennels in front of us to emphasize the point. In response, the dogs started barking and howling.

Dad smiled. "That we do." He checked his watch. "Is that the bus I hear?"

A beep sounded above the sounds of the animals crunching and slurping. "Yikes." I dropped the empty feed scoop I was holding and rushed to grab my school things. "See you later." While I hurried out the door and raced down the long dirt driveway, the bus honked again.

The bus driver frowned at me as I climbed up the bus steps. "Glad you could join us, Ms. Fiol," she said.

"Sorry," I murmured meekly, scooting past her and taking the first empty seat I saw.

As the bus wheezed into gear, I sighed and sank back against the seat. The conversation with Dad kept running through my head.

Why hadn't I just said what I really thought? Obviously my not-so-subtle hints about Penny hadn't sunk in. What was I going to do if Dad called Penny? If he started dating her?

I couldn't even imagine what that would be like. And I really didn't want to find out.

I wasn't in the world's greatest mood when I got to school. I'd spent the entire bus ride trying to figure out what my dad could possibly see in Penny. Unfortunately, I was no closer to an answer than when I started.

When I got to my locker, Traci was there waiting for me.

"Did you practice last night?" she demanded.

I shot her a sour look. "Good morning to you, too," I said, dropping my backpack and flute case on the floor.

Traci stared at me as I spun the combination on my locker. "Are you okay?"

"Not really," I muttered. "Dad just told me he's going to call Penny."

"You mean Amanda's Penny?" Traci looked interested. "What do you mean, call her? Like, ask her out?"

I shrugged. "I guess."

"So what's the problem?" Traci leaned against the locker next to mine and twirled one finger in her pale blond hair. "Penny's awesome. I think they'd make a really cute couple."

"Well, *I* don't," I snapped. Yanking open my locker, I buried my head in it and fished around for my English book.

"Wait a sec," Traci said, poking me on the shoulder until I turned to face her again. "Your parents have been divorced for, like, two years. Haven't they been dating other people?"

"No," I said with a frown. Why did Traci make it sound like that was weird? "And I definitely don't want Dad to start with someone like stupid Penny. They're so totally wrong for each other, it's not even funny. Besides, can you imagine listening to her blab about crystals and stuff all the time? I can hear it now—'Ooh, Luis, you'd better wear this crystal belt buckle I made you. It's so *centering.*'"

For extra emphasis, I did my best to imitate Penny's trilling, high-pitched giggle. I even tossed my head like she does.

When I did, I suddenly noticed Amanda and Arielle standing right behind me. They must have walked up while I was complaining about Penny. And judging from the look on Amanda's face, they must have heard at least some of what I'd said. Including that goofy laugh. Uh-oh.

"Penny doesn't sound like that," Amanda said with a frown.

"Whatever," I said, a little embarrassed that she'd caught me. But it didn't change what I thought. "However she sounds, I don't want my dad dating her."

"Your dad wants to date her?" That shut Amanda up for a few seconds. She didn't sound too happy about it, either. "Oh."

"Wow, that's a surprise," Arielle said with a smirk. "I mean, I'm surprised Penny's crystals didn't predict that all this would happen."

I knew she was sort of joking, but it still made me feel a little better. At least I wasn't the only one who thought Penny was weird. "Yeah," I said with a giggle. "Maybe her crystals could tell us why my dad wants to ask her out in the first place."

Amanda put both hands on her hips. "What's wrong with Penny?" she demanded.

"Let's see—she's annoying, she's obnoxious, she uses words like *okeydokey*. . . ." Arielle jokingly began ticking things off on her fingers.

I could tell that Arielle's comments were making

Amanda mad. Her cheeks were turning pink, and an angry little line was forming between her eyebrows.

Uh-oh. Amanda didn't get upset easily, but when she did, she got *really* upset. And I definitely didn't want her to get mad at me over something so dumb. I almost opened my mouth to apologize—to tell her that Penny really wasn't so bad. At least not when she wasn't putting her hand on my dad's arm and telling embarrassing stories about me.

But I couldn't seem to make the words come out. I was still too upset at the thought of Penny and my dad going out together.

"Anyway, it's not like this will last long," Arielle spoke up again. "None of Penny's romances ever do."

Amanda glared at Arielle, then at me, then at Arielle again. Her cheeks were bright red. "Shut up, you guys!" she cried.

Then she spun on her heel and stomped off.

Traci grimaced as she watched her go. "Yikes," she said. "You guys were kind of harsh. I mean, it's obvious Penny means a lot to Amanda—even I know that, and I just met her yesterday."

"She'll get over it," Arielle said coolly.

Traci scowled at her. "Well, if you two aren't going to go after her, I guess I will."

Before Arielle or I could respond, Traci took off in the direction Amanda had gone.

I frowned. My heart was pounding double time, the

way it always did when there was tension among my friends. What was wrong with me? Why did I have to open my big mouth? Now everything was going to be messed up again.

Still, it wasn't really my fault. It was Penny's. Even Amanda should be able to see that.

Not to mention Traci.

I couldn't believe Traci was taking sides against me—again. The same thing had happened during our first big fight. Traci had ditched me to go along with Amanda. Did she like Amanda better than me now?

"Don't worry about Amanda," Arielle said.

I blinked at her. I'd almost forgotten she was still standing there. "What?"

Arielle shrugged and examined her fingernails, which were painted a cool shade of peach. "Amanda's just extra touchy about Penny today because the two of them were supposed to hang out next weekend. But Penny called Amanda this morning before school to tell her she might not be able to do it after all."

"Oh." I leaned against my locker door and thought about that for a second. I couldn't help wondering exactly what Penny was planning to do next weekend instead of hanging out with Amanda. Was she keeping her schedule open in case my dad called? Or maybe she and my dad had *already* made plans.

I shook my head, feeling totally paranoid. That couldn't be it. Even Penny had to realize that she and my dad had nothing in common. As soon as *he* realized the same thing, this whole problem would go away as fast as it had come. At least I hoped so.

"Anyway, Amanda was kind of worked up about it," Arielle went on. She was still staring at her fingernails, so I guess she didn't see how upset I was. "I tried to tell her to chill. After all, it's not like she's never blown *me* off to go hang with Perky Penny." She rolled her eyes.

"Yeah," I muttered. I was glad that Arielle was taking my side. At least someone understood about Penny.

"Come on, we'd better get moving," I told Arielle. "The first bell is going to ring soon."

Arielle nodded. She headed off down the hall. I grabbed my books, slammed my locker shut, and followed.

"Don't worry too much about Amanda," Arielle advised as we walked down the crowded hallway. "She'll probably forget the whole thing before long, and then—"

"Yo! Davis! What's up?" a voice interrupted.

"Hey, guys," Arielle called back, waving at a group of girls from the soccer team hanging out by the water fountain.

I shifted my books to my other arm and hung back as Arielle hurried over to talk to the group. Like I said, she knows everyone, and everyone knows her. I, on the other hand, might as well be invisible. I leaned uncomfortably against the wall, wondering whether I should wait for Arielle or leave.

Finally, Arielle finished talking to her friends and returned to me. "Did you hear the latest?" she asked excitedly. "We might be having a clinic with some really good soccer players from Europe next month."

"Really? That's great," I said automatically.

"Tell me about it! I'll have to get some new cleats and . . ." She continued chatting about the soccer team as we walked on. It seemed that she'd already forgotten all about Penny, Amanda, and everything else we'd just been talking about.

Lucky her. I couldn't seem to get Penny out of my head. "Um, yeah?" I mumbled when she paused for breath.

She gave me a strange look. "Are you listening to me, Felicia?" she asked.

"Sorry!" I said immediately. "Um, I guess I got distracted there for a second. But I'm listening now. What were you saying?"

Seeming satisfied, she launched into more about soccer. But despite my words, I really wasn't listening. As we walked down the hall, I barely even saw the other kids rushing past in all directions as everyone headed for homeroom. All I could focus on was what had just happened.

It was easy for Arielle to say that Amanda would get over it. The two of them always made up—they'd been friends too long to stay mad at each other. But I'd only really been friends with them for a couple of weeks. What if Amanda decided I wasn't worth the trouble?

I bit my lip, not liking the answer I came up with. It wasn't until Arielle elbowed me in the side that I snapped back to reality.

"Huh?" I said.

"Wake up, Fiol," Arielle said. "We're here."

Glancing around, I realized we were standing in front of Arielle's homeroom. It also happened to be Amanda and Traci's homeroom. I gulped, not sure if I wanted to run into the two of them or not.

"Oops," I told Arielle apologetically. "Sorry, guess I was distracted again."

"It's no big," Arielle said. "You'd better hurry if you want to make the late bell, though."

"Right. See you later," I said, relieved that at least one person wasn't mad at me.

I hurried down the hallway to my homeroom, sliding into my seat just seconds before the late bell rang. As usual, nobody even noticed my entrance. All around me, kids chatted with their friends, laughing and joking, while I sat there feeling invisible. Even the teacher barely glanced at me when she took roll.

Slumping down in my seat, I stared at my desk and waited for the bell to ring. I wondered what my friends were doing in homeroom. Was Amanda still mad at Arielle? Or had they made up already? Were she and Traci talking about me? Was Arielle joining in? What were they saying?

I still couldn't believe how this whole situation had gone so far out of control so fast. Why hadn't I just kept my big mouth shut about Penny? It was bad enough having to deal with the idea of her with my dad. Having to deal with it while my friends were mad at me was a million times worse.

Thinking about that was making my head hurt. Lowering my chin onto my hands, I closed my eyes and did my best not to think about it anymore.

# chapter
## FOUR

**WLMS lunch menu / Tuesday**

```
fish sticks
lima bean and carrot medley
tossed green salad
raisin rolls
milk or juice
fresh grapes
```

```
Bon appétit, students!
```

When the lunch bell rang, I stopped at my locker to drop off my books, then hurried to the cafeteria. As I came out of the lunch line, I saw that Amanda, Arielle, and Traci were already sitting at our usual table by the back windows. My hands started shaking. What should I do now? Just act like nothing was wrong? I wasn't sure I could do that.

I took a few tentative steps toward the table. Amanda looked up, spotted me, and waved.

"Hey, Felicia," she called. "I just wanted to apologize for freaking out on you this morning."

I was so relieved that my knees went weak. Hurrying over, I set down my tray in the empty seat across from her. "I'm sorry, too," I said. "Really, really sorry. I shouldn't have made fun of Penny."

"Well, I shouldn't have overreacted." Amanda smiled and stuck out her hand. "Friends?"

"Friends!" I blurted happily, grabbing her hand and squeezing it. "Definitely!"

I sat down and glanced at my lunch tray. Knowing that Amanda and I were still friends almost made up for the fact that I'd had to buy lunch that day. I'd been so busy in the shelter that morning, I'd totally forgotten today was fish-stick day. I'm not too crazy about fish in any form. Squished into a little log and rolled in greasy breading? Forget about it.

"Ick." Arielle wrinkled her nose and poked tentatively at her food with her fork. "I must have read the menu wrong. I thought today was pizza day."

"Lima beans rule!" a familiar-sounding voice yelled from somewhere nearby.

Glancing over, I saw Ryan Bradley standing on his chair. He was holding up a spoonful of mushy pale green beans with a few sickly orange carrot pieces mixed in. As I watched, he pretended to lose his balance and fall off the chair. On his way down, he managed to dump the vegetables in his friend Trevor's hair.

"Hey!" Trevor leaped to his feet and wiped at his head. In the process, he accidentally mushed one of the lima beans into his ear. Ryan laughed so hard, he almost fell over.

I shuddered and turned back to my friends. Ryan is nice, but he can be kind of immature sometimes. Was Arielle really crushing on him? It hardly seemed possible.

"Anyway," I said to Amanda, "I really am sorry." Thank goodness things were okay between us again. Especially after I'd spent all morning worrying about it.

"It's all right," Amanda said. "It's over."

"I know," I said. But I really wanted her to understand why I'd said those things earlier. I didn't want her to think I was a mean person or anything. "I was just weirded out by seeing her acting that way with my dad. You know, like all *flirty*."

"Uh-huh." Amanda stirred her yogurt. Lucky her—she'd brought her lunch. "I was kind of freaked out, too. I mean, I never would have expected it in a million years."

"Why not?" Arielle put in, spearing a limp piece of lettuce from her salad. "It's not like Penny's a nun or anything."

Amanda stuck out her tongue at her. "Funny. No, I just mean Mr. Fiol isn't exactly the type of man I'd picture Penny with."

It seemed like a totally innocent thing to say, but

49

something about the way she said it made me suspicious. "What do you mean?" I asked cautiously.

"Oh, no offense or anything." Amanda smiled at me. "I just mean that Penny usually dates people who are more like her. You know—artists, or writers, or whatever. Her last boyfriend was this really cool musician. He had a goatee and he played the sitar, which is this Indian instrument, and—"

At that moment, one of the cafeteria's patented rock-hard raisin rolls came flying over our table, almost hitting Traci on the nose.

"Hey!" Traci yelled, standing up and glaring in the direction of Ryan's table. "Cut it out. We're trying to have a civilized lunch over here."

"Sorry!" Ryan called back.

I was so upset, I barely heard the exchange. Just what exactly was Amanda saying about my dad, anyway? She made him sound like some hundred-year-old nerd or something. I might cause more problems, but I didn't want anyone thinking my family was lame.

"You're not saying my dad is too boring to date Penny, are you?" I asked.

Amanda frowned. "Of course not," she replied. "I think your dad is awesome—you know that. He's just not really Penny's type, that's all."

"Oh. Well, Penny's not exactly Dad's type, either," I replied.

That was an understatement. Penny and my dad hardly seemed to be from the same *planet*. I bit back a grimace as I remembered Penny's wacky crystal and her silly laugh.

"That's okay, though, you guys," Traci put in. "They say opposites attract, right?" She smiled hopefully.

"Well, Penny sure is the opposite of Felicia's dad," Arielle said cheerfully. "For instance, Mr. Fiol has an actual job."

"What are you talking about?" Amanda scowled at Arielle. "Penny's art *is* her job. And she takes care of me!"

"Whatever," Traci put in soothingly, shooting Arielle an annoyed glance. "Look, it doesn't matter. They're adults—they'll do what they want to do whether we like it or not. Why stress about it?"

"That's not the point," I said worriedly, thinking back to my conversation with my father that morning. "Dad probably just doesn't realize Penny's all wrong for him yet. I mean, he probably just saw that she's sort of pretty, and when she started giggling and shaking her long blond hair around at him—"

"Hey," Amanda broke in. "It's not like she's some total ditz, you know."

"That's not what I meant." I had to raise my voice a little so my friends could hear me—the shouts coming from the direction of Ryan's table were getting louder and louder. "I just meant he probably isn't really interested in her *personality*, so . . ."

I winced, realizing from the look on Amanda's face that I had said the wrong thing again. My mind raced as I tried to come up with some way to make the situation better.

Just then, Ryan came rushing up to our table, breaking into the tense moment. "Hey," he greeted us breathlessly.

The remains of a lima bean were squished on the front of his purple-and-yellow-striped T-shirt, and a carrot chunk was stuck in his messy brown hair.

"Hi," Traci greeted him. "What are you guys doing over there, anyway? Trying to start a food fight?"

"*Moi?*" Ryan put a hand on his chest, pretending to be insulted. His thumb landed on the squished lima bean. He pulled it away and wiped it off on the edge of our table.

"Eew!" Arielle complained, glaring at Ryan. "Do you mind?" She certainly didn't *look* like she had a crush on him.

Ryan grinned. "Not at all." He leaned on the table. "So anyway, I wanted to tell you guys about Lola's new trick. Felicia's dad taught it to us yesterday at our obedience lesson."

"Really?" Traci asked him.

"Hmmph," Arielle mumbled, sounding disinterested as she picked at her lunch.

Amanda didn't say anything at all. Instead, she just stared down at the table.

Actually, she looked pretty mad. I gulped. Why did I have to be such a spaz? Amanda and I had just made up, and here we were, mad at each other again. All because I was so oversensitive that I thought every little thing was some kind of insult. What was wrong with me? Had Penny's crystal affected my brain or something?

Ryan didn't seem to notice the tension. "Yeah. We taught her to roll over on command. See, that way when she starts to jump up on someone, I can tell her to roll over instead, and it'll distract her so she doesn't jump. That's how it's supposed to work, anyway. . . ."

"That sounds great!" Traci's voice was a little too cheerful. I guess she was trying to lighten the tension between me and Amanda. "Lola is so cute, and she's really smart, too. I'm sure she'll know tons of tricks before long. Maybe you could even start bringing her along on our pet therapy visits."

"Maybe," Ryan said. "But I want to teach her how to skateboard, too. Maybe your brother could help me—he's pretty good on a board."

"I'll ask him," Traci offered.

"Hey, did you guys practice that new orchestra piece much yet?" Ryan asked. "Pretty tough, huh?"

Traci shrugged and stared at her food. Suddenly,

she didn't look so chipper anymore. Was she really that worried about playing the piece? "Yeah," she muttered.

I guess Ryan didn't know what to say after that. So instead of saying anything, he snagged a grape off Arielle's tray and popped it in his mouth. He chewed for a second, then wrinkled his nose.

"Eew!" he cried. "These grapes have seeds in them."

One of Ryan's friends, Jeremy, happened to walk past just then. Ryan turned toward him, pursed his lips, and spit the half-chewed grape right on Jeremy's T-shirt.

"Yo!" Jeremy yelled, jumping back. "You'll pay for that, Bradley."

Ryan grinned. "You'll have to catch me first."

Then he took off, racing back toward his table with Jeremy after him.

I was glad to see them go. Maybe now I could talk to Amanda. It was crazy to let an argument about Penny get in the way of our friendship.

Before I could figure out what to say, Arielle gestured after Ryan and rolled her eyes. "Please," she said. "Is Ryan immature or what?"

Traci frowned slightly. "He's just having fun," she said. "We had food fights at my old school all the time."

"Yeah," Arielle commented. "In *fifth grade*. I guess Ryan thinks he's still back in elementary school."

I still had no idea why Arielle was so obsessed with Ryan all of a sudden, but I was getting tired of it already. We had more important things to talk about.

"Whatever," Traci said shortly. "Hey, Felicia, speaking of orchestra, I heard a lot of people are having trouble with that piece. Maybe if enough of them complain, Mom will realize it's too hard. I mean, did you check out that third stanza? Who does she think we are—like *Mozart* or someone?"

"Uh, yeah. I mean no." I blinked at Traci, then glanced over at Amanda. She was sitting there silently, picking at her food with a cold look on her face.

I opened my mouth, wanting to apologize. But I wasn't sure what to say. Had I really said anything so wrong? All I'd said was Dad couldn't really be interested in Penny's personality. That was just common sense, wasn't it? After all, they'd just met each other. And some people just aren't compatible. That's all there is to it.

*It doesn't matter,* I told myself. *The important thing is making up with Amanda before things get out of control again. And then keeping your big mouth shut about Penny so you don't cause more trouble.*

Easier said than done, though. Amanda was still staring down at her lunch. I guessed she wasn't going to be the first to apologize this time. I gulped and was about to speak when suddenly I felt something hit the back of my arm. Looking down, I saw a big grease stain on my sleeve. A fish-stick stain.

"Yuck!" I cried, spinning around to see where the missile had come from.

One of the boys at Ryan's table whooped and pointed at me. He scooped up another fish stick and aimed it my way.

"Look out!" Arielle cried.

We all ducked. The fish stick flew over our heads and hit a passing girl on the forehead. The boys at Ryan's table cheered loudly.

The girl screamed, then scooped up a handful of lima beans and carrots from the tray she was holding. Dropping the tray at the end of our table, she raced toward the boys.

"Uh-oh," Traci commented. "This doesn't look too good."

I glanced over at the teachers' table near the door. For some reason, the only one there today was Mr. Reid, my weirdo math teacher. He was staring over his shoulder at our end of the room, looking confused.

Ryan was standing on his chair again. He pumped his fist—which happened to be dripping with squished lima beans—in the air.

"Food fight!" he yelled.

"Let's get out of here!" Arielle yelped, already jumping to her feet.

She was right. Our table was way too close to the

war zone. Just as we started to gather our things, two more raisin rolls came flying over and one pelted Arielle in the arm.

"Hey, enough!" she yelled at Ryan, but he was too busy flinging fish sticks to notice. She shook her head and grabbed her book bag. "Time to bail. Later, guys."

As a spoonful of lima beans headed toward our table, the four of us scattered. I tried to follow Traci and Amanda, but the food fight was so intense, I lost sight of them and had to fend for myself.

I ended up hiding behind the garbage cans, watching the raisin rolls and fish sticks fly.

I sighed, wondering where Amanda had gone. Thanks to Ryan and his immature food fights, I'd lost my big chance to try to make things right with Amanda.

Mr. Reid was running toward the heart of the action, shouting at the top of his lungs about month-long detentions, and one of the cafeteria ladies was banging on a frying pan with a big metal spoon. But it was pretty hopeless. The food fight was already as far out of control as the whole ridiculous Penny situation.

*Oh, well*, I told myself, ducking as a grape came whizzing over my head. *I guess I'll just have to talk to Amanda after school. Maybe by then I'll know what to say.*

I managed to escape from the cafeteria, then spent the next few classes totally distracted. All I could think about was how awful it would be if my friends and I didn't make up soon. What if we *never* made up? What if the others decided it wasn't worth it—that being my friend and having all these arguments was too much trouble?

That idea kept my stomach churning all through my math and Spanish classes. Now that I'd had a couple of weeks of having great friends, suddenly the idea of not having them seemed like the worst thing in the entire universe. I'd felt the same way during our first fight. But this one seemed even worse somehow. Maybe because it was mostly my fault.

Unfortunately, by the time orchestra practice rolled around, I still had no idea what to do to fix things with Amanda. When I walked into the music room, Traci was already seated, warming up by playing some scales. She looked uncomfortable.

"Hey," I greeted her tentatively as I took my seat in the flute section.

She glanced up at me. "Hey," she replied softly.

She didn't return my smile. That was bad news. Traci is one of those people who almost always has a smile on her face, unless she's really upset or mad about something. I wondered if that meant she was mad at me because of what had happened at lunch, but I was kind of afraid to ask.

Sitting down in my seat in the flute section, I opened my case and started putting together my flute. As I glanced over toward Traci again, wondering whether to try to talk to her some more, I saw Ryan Bradley slide into the seat next to her.

"What did you think of the food fight today?" he asked loudly, poking her on the shoulder. "Pretty funny, huh?"

Traci rolled her eyes at him and laughed. "Yeah, I could tell Mr. Reid thought it was hysterical."

"I know." Ryan grinned. "He looked pretty dumb with that fish stick in his hair."

I bit my lip as the two of them continued to kid around. So Traci couldn't even manage a smile for me, but she was obviously in a good enough mood to joke around with goofy Ryan. How weird was that?

Luckily Ms. McClintic came in before I could worry about it too much. "Okay, people," she said, clapping. "Let's start with some warm-up scales."

We started to play. The scales were easy, but I still felt distracted—I kept looking over at Traci, wondering what she was thinking. Why did she seem upset?

After we finished the scales, Ms. McClintic pulled out the music for the new piece.

"Uh-oh, here goes nothing," Ryan quipped loudly as he raised his violin to his chin.

There were a few nervous giggles from around the

room. This time Traci wasn't smiling, though. She shot Ryan a nervous glance and licked her lips.

I knew how she felt.

"Very funny, Mr. Bradley," Ms. McClintic said with a slight smile. "Now, I know this piece is challenging, but I also know you all can do it. Let's take it from the top."

She counted off, and we started to play. The flute part was fairly easy at the beginning, but I still had trouble hitting the right notes. My mind kept drifting back to my own problems, and my fingers felt like they had a mind of their own. I blushed as I totally fumbled a simple glissando. Luckily, the brass section was playing the main part at that point, so I don't think anyone even noticed my mistake.

Then we reached a new section of the piece. That was when the clarinets and violins took over the melody. The brass players dropped out completely for a few bars, and we flutes just had to play an easy counter-melody. Even in my distracted state, I was pretty sure I could manage that.

The section started well. The violins, led by Ryan, picked up the melody first. Then it was time for the clarinets to enter.

I saw Traci take a deep breath and move her fingers. I felt really nervous for her. The next thing I knew, there was a loud squawk from her direction. I mean, *really* loud.

"It's okay, Traci," Ms. McClintic called, still directing the rest of the orchestra as we continued to play. "Find your place and pick it up again."

Traci's cheeks turned pink as she glanced quickly at her mother, then around the room. Her gaze met mine for a split second before bouncing away. But that was enough time for me to see the look of total humiliation in her eyes. I wasn't surprised. Traci is really good—she almost never makes huge mistakes like that in orchestra.

I heard a few muffled snorts coming from the string section. Glancing over, I saw that Ryan was shaking with laughter. Still, he was managing not to miss a note. It figured that he would think it was hysterical for someone to mess up.

But I didn't waste much time thinking about him. I was too busy feeling sorry for Traci—and for myself. She was too good a player to be having that much trouble without a really good reason. Obviously, she was upset about our fight, too. So upset that she couldn't even play right.

Tears sprang to my eyes, blurring the notes on the sheet music in front of me. The past day and a half already felt like a long, horrible lifetime. Were things ever going to go back to normal for me and my friends?

# chapter
## FIVE

**Note left on the Fiols' refrigerator door:**

Dear Felicia,

Hope orchestra practice went well! I'm over at Penny's house—she invited us both for dinner, and I promised to bring by some ingredients she needs for her world-famous chili. I'll be home at five o'clock to pick you up. Make sure you put on some nice clothes, okay, sweetie?

Love, Dad

*Clunk!*

I was so surprised by Dad's note that I dropped my flute case. Penny's house? *Penny's house?* Was he for real? Orchestra practice had been painful enough. After Ms. McClintic had dismissed us, Traci had scooted from the room so fast that I hadn't had a chance to try to talk to her. So basically, I still had no idea if I had any friends left. And now I was supposed to go eat chili with the woman who had started all our problems?

I read the note again. I couldn't believe Dad was serious about this. And since when did he call me "sweetie"? He wasn't really the nickname type. Usually, he just calls me "Felicia." Or sometimes, when he's in a really wacky mood, "daughter of mine."

Gnawing on my thumbnail, I read the note one more time. This was unbelievable. Totally, completely unbelievable.

"Ugh," I muttered out loud. "If I have to eat dinner with that ditz, I'll probably get sick to my stomach."

I blinked, thinking about what I'd just said. Hmmm. Maybe that was the easiest way out of all this. I could say I didn't feel well, Dad would come home, and that would be that.

I was excited for a second. Then I came to my senses. Dad wasn't going to believe I'd suddenly come down with the flu at school. No way. I was going to need a better excuse than that to get him to stay home.

I gnawed on my thumbnail some more. I needed to come up with a story before Dad got home to pick me up. Something really convincing. Something that would make Dad forget all about Penny.

Just then, I heard the sound of faint barking coming from the kennel. Of course! The answer was so obvious. I could say that one of the animals was sick. All I had to do was come up with some convincing symptoms, and Dad would forget Penny ever existed.

Okay, maybe not *forget*. But he definitely wouldn't go back to her house for dinner tonight, either. Not even if the animal didn't look sick when he got to it. He would still want to keep an eye on it just in case.

It could work. And maybe it would give Dad a chance to realize that things weren't going to work out with Penny. What future could he have with someone who was afraid of dogs, anyway?

I didn't like the idea of lying to my father. But what could I do? It was either that or end up spending a whole evening with him and Penny. Gag.

At five minutes to five, I heard the dogs in the kennel start to bark. A few seconds later, I heard the sound of a motor out front. Our driveway is on a hill, and Dad's old blue van always sounds like it's going to break down by the time it chug-chugs up to the house.

"Here goes nothing," I muttered, hurrying toward the front door.

I was so busy rehearsing what I was going to say that I didn't even look at the van until I was almost on top of it. When I did, I almost had a heart attack. Dad was in the driver's seat.

And Penny was sitting next to him!

"Hi, Felicia!" she trilled, leaning out the passenger-side window. Her crystal necklace caught the light of the afternoon sun and bounced it toward me. I blinked at the sudden flash. Great.

"Hi," I said, realizing that Penny was still staring at me. Suddenly, everything I'd planned to say flew right out of my head.

Meanwhile Dad was climbing out of the driver's side. "I just need to check on the critters. Be right back, you two!" he called before disappearing around the corner of the house.

I gulped and glanced at Penny out of the corner of my eye. She was grinning at me like I was her long-lost best friend.

"So, Felicia," she said cheerfully. "I hope you like chili, because I made a whole trough of it!"

"Um, sure, I guess," I mumbled.

If Penny noticed that my response was less than enthusiastic, she didn't let on. "Wonderful!" she cried. "We're going to have such a nice time tonight, sweetie. I've been hoping for a chance to get to know you."

I wasn't sure what to say to that. Why did she care? Luckily, Dad hurried back around the corner of the house at that moment. "Okeydokey," he called, and I cringed. "Everything looks fine in the shelter, so we can hit the road." I was still standing beside the van, so he patted me on the back. "Why don't you go ahead and hop in the back, sweetie?"

I shuddered. Okeydokey? Sweetie? Who *was* this

pod person, anyway? It certainly couldn't be my dad.

As usual, a cloud of dust and dog hair poufed up from the van's backseat when I sat down. I coughed.

"Cover your mouth, Felicia," Dad said sternly. "Manners, please."

Okay. So maybe it *was* my dad. But he was definitely acting weird.

He started up the van, and we were on our way. Soon Dad and Penny were talking and laughing as if they'd totally forgotten I was there. I didn't mind, though. I wasn't exactly dying to chat with them at the moment.

I slumped against the backseat of the van. There was a huge rip in the vinyl seat cover where a rowdy Rottweiler had once treated it like a chew toy, and the stiff fabric was poking me in the neck. But I hardly noticed.

Why hadn't I just gone ahead with my plan? With Penny here, it could have worked out even better. I could imagine it now—

```
  Me: [worriedly] Dad, I—I think there's some-
      thing wrong with one of the animals. It's
      that huge German shepherd mix. You know,
      the one we call Fang?
 Dad: [anxious] Oh no. What's wrong with Fang?
Penny: [nervous] Fang?
  Me: [ignoring Penny] When I went to check on
```

that cat, I noticed that Fang was sort of
drooling and looking weird.

Dad: *[already heading for the shelter]* Uh-oh.
I'd better take a look.

Me: *[helpfully]* Do you want me and Penny to
hold him down for you? I forgot to tell
you, he's kind of jumping around and
growling, too.

Penny: *[faints]*

Dad: *[disgusted]* Well, a lot of help she turned
out to be. Call her a taxi, please, Felicia.
And if she wakes up before it gets here,
tell her I never want to see her again.

Me: Of course! Anything to help out. . . .

I awoke from my fantasy to realize that Penny was
twisted around in her seat, staring at me. Smiling that
goofy smile of hers.

"Um, what?" I said, guessing that she'd asked me a
question or something. Seeing Dad shoot me a look in
the rearview mirror, I cleared my throat. "Er, I mean,
pardon me?"

"I just wondered, do you take art with Amanda at
school?" Penny asked brightly.

I shrugged. "Not exactly," I muttered.

"What was that, honey?" Dad called from the
front. "I couldn't hear you."

"I said, not exactly," I repeated loudly.

Dad glanced at me in the rearview mirror, looking stern. I realized that answer wasn't going to fly.

"Um, I mean, I do take art," I told Penny grudgingly. "But I'm not in Amanda's class."

My stomach grumbled hungrily. It was so loud, I was surprised Dad and Penny didn't hear it. I realized I hadn't really eaten much of anything since breakfast, thanks to the gross cafeteria food and the food fight. At least maybe I would get a good meal out of this nightmare. That was the only bright side possible.

"I see," Penny said cheerfully. "And do you enjoy it?"

"I guess," I murmured.

"What was that, Felicia?" Dad asked in his "warning" tone.

I cleared my throat. "I like it, but it's not my favorite class or anything."

"Oh." Penny smiled. "So, what is your favorite class, sweetie?"

I cringed. I really, really, really wished she would stop calling me that.

"Um, I don't know," I said. "I guess lunch."

Penny laughed, and Dad chuckled, too. I frowned. It wasn't really meant to be a joke. Wasn't it kind of rude to laugh at someone you didn't know that well? So why wasn't Dad shooting Penny any warning looks?

"That was always my favorite, too," Penny said

when she stopped laughing. "Well, along with art class. And a few extracurriculars. I also always loved doing volunteer work. I guess that's another thing we have in common, right, Felicia?"

"What do you mean?" I asked cautiously.

"Amanda has been telling me all about your new pet therapy visits," Penny explained. "It sounds like a lot of fun."

"We don't do it because it's fun," I said stiffly. "We do it to help people."

This time Dad was the one who burst out laughing. "Okay, sweetie," he said jokingly. "We'll just have to start calling you Mother Felicia."

Penny giggled. "Mother Felicia—I like it!" She winked at me.

My face flamed. How could Dad make fun of me like that in front of Penny? Was this another weird personality change? I couldn't help noticing that he was laughing an awful lot. Not that he's serious all the time, but he doesn't usually giggle nonstop like some crazed cheerleader, either.

It was like he became a completely different person whenever Penny was around. And he didn't even seem to notice.

"Oh, look," Penny exclaimed brightly as Dad pulled into a driveway. "There's Amanda."

"Huh?" I sat up and looked out the car window.

Amanda was pacing back and forth at the top of the

driveway. She was wearing one of her long, flowy, hippie-style skirts that waved out behind her as she walked.

Penny twisted around to smile at me again. "It's a special surprise," she explained. "I thought it would be nice to ask Amanda to dinner, too, since you two are such good friends."

"Oh." I gulped. That was a surprise, all right. It would be even more surprising if Amanda was still talking to me.

I guess Penny's plan was a surprise to Amanda, too. She frowned when she saw me climb out of the van.

"Oh," she said, looking confused. "What are *you* doing here?"

"Surprise!" Penny cried, jumping out of the passenger seat and hurrying over to give Amanda a hug. "Isn't this great, sweetie? Instead of a boring night eating pizza and cleaning paintbrushes, we're having a little dinner party!"

"Great." Amanda smiled at Penny. The smile looked totally fake to me, but Penny didn't seem to notice. She'd already turned to take my dad by the arm.

"Come on, Luis," she said. "Let's give Felicia the grand tour."

"Sure." Dad glanced at me. "Wait until you see Penny's sculptures, Felicia. You'll love them."

I wasn't too sure about that. So far I didn't *love* anything about Penny.

I trailed behind as the two adults hurried toward the house, and Amanda fell into step beside me. For one brief, optimistic second I thought maybe she wanted to make up for the misunderstanding at lunch.

"Penny was supposed to be hanging out with *me* tonight," she hissed. "I thought you didn't even like her."

My heart sank. So she *was* mad at me. Now what was I supposed to do?

"It wasn't my idea to come here—it was hers," I said.

I was just trying to explain why I was there so Amanda didn't think I was being two-faced or something. But I guess it didn't come out quite the way I meant it because Amanda just scowled in response.

Before I could come up with a better way to explain, Penny turned around and waved at us. "Hurry up, girls!" she cried. "The chili will be ready in fifteen minutes, so there's not much time for the tour."

For the next few minutes, Amanda and I didn't have a chance to talk at all. We followed Penny around as she showed off her house, yard, and studio. I wasn't really paying that much attention, but I had to admit the place was pretty nice. The house didn't look like much from the street—just your average white two-story house. But inside, each room was painted a different color. There was art everywhere—not just Penny's, but paintings and photos and sculptures by all kinds of different people.

Her studio was a huge, sunny room built off the back of the house. It had white walls, giant skylights, and wide wooden floorboards. Several of Penny's creations were scattered around—a red-white-and-blue elephant, a giant pair of red sneakers, and even a plain old woman's head that was normal colors and everything. The studio's floor-to-ceiling windows overlooked a garden filled with plants. There were also a couple more sculptures out there, including a bronze statue of a dog chasing a butterfly.

"Hey," I blurted when I saw it. "I thought you hated dogs."

"What?" Penny followed my gaze to the sculpture. "Oh. No, I don't hate them. Not at all." Her voice was much more subdued than usual. "I just enjoy them from a distance, that's all."

"Yeah," Amanda put in defensively. "Nothing wrong with that."

I winced. Did Amanda have to jump all over *everything* I said? No wonder we hadn't managed to make up yet.

Dad patted Penny on the back. "It's okay," he said. "A lot of people are nervous around dogs."

Penny smiled at him gratefully. Then she glanced over at me again. "Oh! That reminds me," she exclaimed, hurrying toward a large pine cabinet against one wall of the studio. "Come here, Felicia."

What now? I took a step toward her as she rummaged in the cabinet.

She turned around a second later with something in her hand. "Here," she said, "this is for you."

Before I could move, she rushed over and pressed something into my hand. I looked at it. It was a bracelet. Most of it was made of small, round, greenish blue beads. There were a few larger silvery beads here and there, and in the middle was a big, flat white bead. It seemed to have something painted on it, but I didn't look that closely. I was too surprised. Why was Penny giving me this?

"It's a gift," Penny said expectantly when I didn't say anything for a few seconds.

"Oh. Um, that's okay," I blurted. "You don't have to give me anything." I tried to shove it back at her.

"But I want you to have it," Penny insisted.

Seeing that Dad was glaring at me warningly again, I shrugged. "Okay, thanks," I mumbled. "It's nice."

Penny smiled, seeming pleased. "I'm glad you like it."

"Why don't you try it on, Felicia?" Dad suggested.

I slipped it onto my wrist. Did I have a choice? "It matches my shirt," I said weakly.

"Yes, it's lovely," Dad said. "I'm sure Felicia will wear it often, Penny."

Amanda held up her arm. As usual, there were

74

about ten bracelets on it. I noticed that one of them looked a lot like the one Penny had just given me.

"Look, Mr. Fiol," Amanda said brightly. "Penny gave me a beautiful bracelet—it has my name painted on it, see? Actually, she's given me all kinds of cool stuff. A necklace with a crystal she brought back from Tibet, some painted T-shirts, a sculpture of a seagull, and tons of other stuff. A lot of people would be jealous of all the Penny Zinsser originals I have. I mean, Penny's a pretty famous artist around here—she had her own gallery show and was written up in the *Gazette* and everything."

"All right, Amanda." Penny smiled at her. "If you don't cut it out, I'm going to have to fire my agent and hire you instead."

Dad chuckled. "Is our fifteen minutes up?" he asked, checking his watch. "I think I smell something delicious."

"Oh! I'd better go check on the chili." Penny patted Amanda on the shoulder. "Could you show the Fiols to the dining room, sweetie?"

"Of course!" Amanda said. "No problem. I know this house like my own—because I spend so much time here."

Penny hurried ahead. Dad followed more slowly with Amanda, asking her something about school.

I lagged behind. Soon they'd all disappeared into the hall beyond the studio.

I leaned against a polka-dotted horse, relieved to have a moment of privacy. This evening was turning into a nightmare.

For one thing, Amanda was acting like a total freak. It wasn't like her. Usually, she was the last person to pick a fight with anyone. But now it seemed like she was looking for any excuse to get mad at me and stay that way.

Then there was Dad. He still didn't seem to notice how weird this all was. Not to mention how weird *Penny* was.

Penny. She was the biggest problem of all, of course. She was acting like my new best friend, and I didn't like it. I didn't like *her*. It was so obvious—she was just being nice to me so my dad would like her better. Why else would she give me a present?

That reminded me about the bracelet. I couldn't resist giving it a closer look. Holding up my arm, I saw that there was a dog painted on the white bead. It looked sort of like this dog named Ragu, a chocolate Lab we'd adopted out about a month earlier.

As I was staring at it, Penny hurried back in and caught me. "Oh," she said softly. "There you are. I hope you like the bracelet. Your father said you've always enjoyed playing with the dogs at the shelter."

That gave me an idea. "Oh, I do," I said, glancing past her to make sure my dad was nowhere in sight. "I get my love of dogs from Dad. He's *crazy* about them. All of them. Even the big, tough ones."

"Really." Penny looked interested.

"Yeah," I said. "He spends as much time with them as he possibly can. He even brings them in from the shelter to sleep with him at night. Right in his bed."

That wasn't exactly true. But he'd once brought in Lucy the dachshund for a couple of nights when she was sick. He'd made up a basket at the foot of the bed so he could hear if she cried.

Penny wasn't smiling for once. "Really," she said again.

"Uh-huh." I crossed my fingers behind my back. I didn't like lying, but I was desperate. "He also never showers without a dog in there to keep him company. And he likes to let them sit on the table while we eat dinner. Well, the smaller ones, anyway. The big ones just lie around under the table. Sometimes we'll have twenty dogs in the kitchen with us."

At that moment, Dad appeared around the corner. I guess he'd heard some of what I was saying because he was frowning.

"Now, Felicia," he said. "Don't exaggerate. The most dogs we've ever had in the kitchen was four, and those were the orphan puppies that needed to be fed around the clock."

"Sorry," I mumbled. "I guess it just seemed like twenty."

Penny laughed. "Puppies? How adorable." She gestured to us. "Come on. The food is ready."

Rats. Another plan shot down. But maybe my stories had given Penny an idea of what kind of person Dad was. True, he didn't sleep and eat and shower with dogs, but he did spend an awful lot of time with them. And any woman who wanted to be with him needed to realize that.

It was just another way that Penny and Dad were all wrong for each other. All I had to do was find a way to make them see it.

# chapter SIX

**Wonder Lake Gazette, Features section:**

LOCAL ARTIST GOES WILD AT WONDER LAKE GALLERY

Is the Wonder Lake Gallery being taken over by purple penguins and chartreuse sheep? Yes, but only from now until the eighteenth. After that, the art show by local talent Penelope Zinsser will, sadly, be only a memory to her many fans.

Ms. Zinsser, who lives in the Green Hills section of town, has been creating her unique creatures for more than ten years. A graduate of the Johnson School of Art, she specializes in papier-mâché sculpture.

"I love following my imagination, creating an animal or person who is lifelike, yet whimsical," Ms. Zinsser explained in a recent interview. "That makes my work a lot more fun."

The results are a lot of fun for art lovers as well. Come on down to the Wonder Lake Gallery and see for yourself!

"Voilà! Dinner is served," Penny announced as she swept the lid off a large crockpot with a flourish.

"Felicia? Can I serve you up some of my world-famous vegetarian chili?"

Vegetarian? I froze in the act of handing over my bowl. "Um, what's in it?" I asked.

Dad shot me a warning look. "I'm sure it's very good, Felicia."

"Yes, I'll bet," I said, trying to sound sincere. Dad would kill me if I was really rude. "Um, what do you put in vegetarian chili?"

Penny seemed thrilled that I'd asked. "Oh, it's my own special recipe," she said. "There are plenty of yummy beans, of course. And chili peppers and tomatoes. Then, instead of adding meat, I just throw in a few more good things from the farmer's market— some zucchini and a few big juicy carrots, an eggplant or two . . ."

I gulped, feeling my stomach flip over. Eggplant. I hated eggplant. I couldn't even stand to smell it, let alone taste it.

Dad gave me another stern glance. He knew all about my eggplant phobia. "I'm sure it's delicious, Penny. I can't wait to try it."

I happened to know that he wasn't crazy about eggplant, either. But he didn't mention that. Of course.

"None for me, thanks," I said. "I'm not very hungry."

That was a lie. My stomach was so empty, I was afraid it was going to start eating itself. Luckily, there was a basket of corn muffins on the table along with the chili. I grabbed for one of the muffins just as Amanda reached for the basket.

"Excuse me," she muttered, snatching her hand back so fast, she almost knocked over her water glass.

I didn't know what to say. Grabbing a muffin, I stuffed half of it in my mouth so I wouldn't have to talk at all. There were little chunks of some kind of vegetable in the muffins. I wasn't sure what they were, but they weren't eggplant, and that was all that mattered.

"Mmm," Amanda said, licking her lips as she helped herself to some chili. "Your vegetarian chili looks delicious, just like always, Penny."

"Don't forget to try one of the corn-pumpkin muffins, Amanda," Penny chirped. "It's a new recipe, and I think they turned out pretty well."

"Pumpkin?" Amanda said. She shot me a look. "Um, okay. I'm sure they're great."

Penny smiled. "I know pumpkin isn't your favorite, Amanda, but you can barely taste it in this recipe."

If I wasn't in such a bad mood, I would have laughed. I happen to know that Amanda *hates* pumpkin. She just about gagged when the cafeteria served pumpkin pie for dessert one day. She couldn't even stand to watch while Traci ate hers. What were the odds that Penny would make both of our least-favorite foods in one meal?

Amanda didn't look amused. She just started eating her chili. My dad, too, was busy shoveling spoonful after spoonful into his mouth.

"This chili is great, Penny," he gushed. I guess the eggplant wasn't bothering *him*. "Amanda, you're really lucky to have a master chef cooking some of your meals."

Amanda nodded, beaming.

I couldn't believe Dad was acting like this. I was ready to gag.

I distracted myself by wondering what was wrong with me. Why couldn't I figure out a way to make things right with Amanda? It shouldn't be that hard. Amanda is one of the most forgiving people I've ever met, not to mention one of the sweetest and most understanding. So why was she so mad at me?

Well, I guess the answer was obvious. It was all Penny's fault.

"Felicia? Felicia! Wake up!"

I jumped. Dad was staring at me from the other end of the table.

"What?" I blurted.

"Penny just asked you a question," Dad replied sternly. "The least you could do is pay attention, after all the trouble she went to making us this nice meal."

"It's okay, Luis," Penny broke in soothingly. "She's just daydreaming. I completely understand—I do that a lot myself."

She smiled at me. Dad was watching, so I forced a small, fake grin in return.

I was so on to her. She was trying to make it sound like she had something in common with me. She probably thought that would make Dad like her better. And the way things were going, maybe she was right.

"Anyway, Felicia, I was just asking how you like working with animals," Penny went on. "Are you a lifelong animal lover like your dad?"

"I guess," I replied. "I mean, we've always had animals around even before Dad opened the shelter. Mom used to call our house the Fiol Zoo."

As soon as the words left my mouth, I felt my face go bright red. Still, why shouldn't I mention Mom? I wondered what she would think of Penny and of this weird "dinner party." Penny seemed to be about as different from Mom as you could get.

"Felicia is a great help at the shelter," Dad told Penny, reaching over to help himself to another muffin. "Her friends come by after school to volunteer, too, as you know. Amanda here is one of my best workers." He smiled at her.

"Thanks, Mr. Fiol," Amanda said politely. "I really enjoy working with the animals."

I couldn't help being a little hurt at the way she said it. Like the only reason she came over to our house was to see the animals—like I didn't even matter.

Penny stirred her chili. "So what's your favorite animal, Felicia?"

I shrugged. "I don't really have a favorite," I mumbled.

What was with all her questions? Couldn't she tell I didn't want to talk to her?

Maybe that was just it, I realized. Maybe she was afraid that if I didn't like her, Dad wouldn't like her, either. If only it was that easy.

"Oh, come on, Felicia," Dad prompted. "What about Lola? I thought she was the big favorite with all you girls." He turned to Penny. "I'm sure Amanda told you about her. She's this cute pup that the girls' friend Ryan adopted recently. Oh, and then there was the cute little Siamese cat we placed last month . . ."

I tuned him out as he started running through the shelter's greatest hits. Penny looked really interested, but I was sure she was faking it. It was so obvious that Dad and Penny were all wrong for each other. Why couldn't they see it?

I had to do something about it. It was obvious that Amanda wasn't exactly thrilled about Dad and Penny's new relationship, either. Maybe if I talked to her about it, she would see that we were really on the same side. Then we could work together to do something to fix it.

"Hey, Penny?" Amanda started. "Did you read that article in the *Wonder Lake Gazette*, about the school maybe cutting arts funding?"

Penny nodded, losing her smile for the first time the whole dinner. "Yes, I did," she said. "It's a real tragedy. Arts are an important part of a well-rounded education, don't you think, Luis?"

I looked at my dad. He'd never so much as picked up a crayon as long as I could remember. "Absolutely," he said.

"I wish there was something I could do," Amanda said. "Maybe we'll talk about it at our next student government meeting."

Penny beamed at her. "I think it's great that you're getting involved, Amanda," she said. "When you make your voice heard, you can really make a difference."

Amanda looked like she would burst with pride. "I hope so."

Then Penny turned to me again. "How about you, Felicia?" she asked, tearing off a piece of muffin. "Are you involved in student government?"

I shrugged and took another bite of muffin, thinking about how great a hamburger would taste right now. "No."

"Felicia's not much of a politician." My dad caught

my eye and winked at me. "She's more of a creative type. A musician."

Penny looked so excited, you'd think he had just told her I'd won the Nobel Prize. "Really?" Penny smiled. "Well, I can identify with being a creative type, sweetie. What do you play?"

"The flute." I tried to look unenthused. I didn't want Penny to start thinking we were so alike. I liked playing in the orchestra, but I wasn't going to be playing any songs about purple moose or whatever.

"Well, that's fantastic." Penny turned back to her chili, still smiling. On the other side of the table, Amanda looked unhappy. She was probably upset that I'd taken attention away from her talk about student government. I wanted to tell her it was no big deal. The way orchestra was going lately, none of us were going to be great musicians. Except maybe Ryan.

Was that why Arielle was so into him? No, she didn't play in the orchestra. What was it, then? It was all so weird.

The meal was winding down. Finally, Penny stood up and started collecting dishes. "Want to help me clear the table, Amanda?"

"That's okay." Dad jumped to his feet. "I'll do it."

Penny beamed at Dad. "Thanks, Luis. In that case, maybe the girls can go out back and bring the beach chairs out of the shed. It's a lovely clear night tonight—I thought we could all sit outside and look at the stars while we chat. Amanda, you can show Felicia where the shed is."

"Sure." Amanda didn't sound thrilled about that. She turned to leave without even looking at me.

Maybe this was my chance. "So," I said tentatively as Amanda and I walked down a long hallway leading toward the back of the house. "Um, this is weird, huh?"

"Definitely," Amanda snapped.

Yikes. I cleared my throat and tried again. "So listen," I said. "Maybe we should try to work together here. You know—to stop this."

Amanda shrugged as she opened the back door. "Stop what?"

I followed her outside. "Stop Dad and Penny from getting together, of course."

"Why?" Amanda glared at me as she swung open the door to a little wooden shed built into the wall beside the back door. "Don't you think Penny is good enough for your father?"

I gritted my teeth. Not this again. "It's not that," I said. "I just think things would be better if they went back to the way they were. I mean, come on, don't you agree?"

Amanda shrugged, not meeting my eyes. She dragged a few aluminum beach chairs out of the shed and dropped them on the lawn.

Before I could figure out what to say next, Dad and

Penny walked through the back door. Both of them were holding mugs, and I could smell the strong scent of coffee. Penny was laughing, and Dad was grinning from ear to ear.

"Oh, good," Penny trilled when she spotted us. "You got the chairs out."

Dad set down his coffee cup and started unfolding the beach chairs. Penny pointed out her favorite spot near a rosebush, and he set up three of the chairs there.

When Dad picked up the fourth chair, Amanda looked at me uncomfortably and cleared her throat. "Listen, Penny," she blurted. "I just realized I have to get back home. I have an English paper due tomorrow."

"Oh." Penny seemed disappointed. "Well, all right, then. I'm glad you could come for dinner."

Amanda smiled weakly. "Yeah, me, too," she said. "Thanks."

"See you at the shelter, Amanda," Dad added.

"Uh-huh. Bye." Amanda waved vaguely toward Dad. She didn't even glance at me as she hurried off toward her house.

I knew she was lying about the English paper. We were in the same class, and the only homework we had was to memorize our vocabulary list.

Of course, I wouldn't mind leaving, either, but when I glanced over at Dad, he didn't look like he was ready to go anytime soon. He was lounging in his chair, sipping his coffee and staring up at the sky.

With a sigh, I flopped down in one of the empty chairs. Penny sat in the other one. "So, Felicia!" she said brightly. "Tell me more about yourself, sweetie. What do you like to do with your time besides take care of animals?"

More questions. "I don't know," I said cautiously. "Lots of stuff."

Penny sipped her coffee and then smiled at me. "Oh?" she said. "Like what? Do you like to read?"

I shrugged. "Sure, I guess."

"She loves to read," Dad put in, leaning over to pat me on the knee. "She spends more time at the library than she does at home."

That wasn't exactly true. I hadn't really hung out at the library since I was about eight years old.

"And what else?" Penny was still staring at me as if I were the most fascinating person on the planet.

"I don't know," I mumbled again, picking at a loose piece of plastic on my beach chair.

What was her problem, anyway? I wasn't sure why she had been giving me the third degree all night, but I didn't like it.

"Do you like playing in the orchestra?" Penny prompted. "Music is such an enriching hobby."

"I'm not that good," I said shortly.

Dad shot me a warning glance.

"That reminds me," he said. "We should probably

be running along so Felicia can practice her flute before bedtime. She tells me she's working on a difficult piece."

Why was he talking about me like I wasn't even there? Oh well, at least we were leaving.

"Oh! So soon?" Penny said. She sounded really disappointed. "Well, I'm glad you could come."

We all stood up. Dad started to fold up his chair, but Penny waved him off. So we all walked toward the van, which was parked in the driveway at the side of the house.

"Thank you so much for the dinner, Penny," Dad said as we walked. "It was delicious."

He raised one eyebrow at me. I knew that look.

"Um, yeah," I muttered. "Thanks for dinner. I liked the pumpkin muffins." *But I would've liked a hamburger better.*

"Oh, I'm so glad!" Penny beamed at me. "And I really enjoyed getting to know you better, Felicia. Feel free to stop by anytime to hang out with Amanda and me. We always have lots of fun, and we'd love to have you join us."

*As if,* I thought, managing to force out a smile.

The van wasn't locked, so I mumbled one last good-bye and bolted for the passenger seat, slamming the door behind me. Dad hung around on the driveway with Penny for a few more seconds. I couldn't hear what they were saying, but I heard Penny's laugh as they shook hands.

Finally, Dad climbed into the driver's seat. Penny stood in the driveway, waving like a maniac as we pulled out. I breathed a sigh of relief as we headed down the street.

Slumping back against the seat, I stared out the window. I couldn't help noticing that Dad was humming under his breath.

"So," he said a couple of blocks later. "That was nice, wasn't it?"

He seemed to be expecting an answer. I shrugged. "I guess."

"I think Penny really likes you, Felicia," he went on. "What do you think of her?"

I knew he wouldn't like my answer to that. So I didn't say anything.

"Felicia?" Dad's voice sounded a little more stern. "I asked you a question."

Oops.

"Sorry," I said quickly. "Um, my stomach hurts a little. I think it was those muffins."

Dad shot me a worried frown before returning his gaze to the road. He didn't look too convinced. But he nodded and kept quiet for the rest of the drive.

Except for the humming, of course.

When we pulled into the driveway, Dad stopped the car and glanced at his watch. "It's getting late," he said. "You'd better get started on your homework. I'm going to run out and check on the animals. I'll be back in a little while."

"Okay," I said.

I wished I could call Arielle. She was the only one who might understand what a rotten night I'd just had. But then I had a sudden flash of inspiration. What if I called my mom instead? Surely, she would understand how weird it was to watch Dad with Penny. She would be worried about the fights I was having with my friends. Quietly, I took the phone into my room and dialed my mom's number. It was eight-fifteen—just in time to catch her before she went to bed. My mom had to get up super early to start working in the bakery, so her bedtime was even earlier than mine.

"Hello?" Hearing my mom's voice calmed me down right away. Good old reliable Mom. I almost wished I was with her right then, curled up on the couch and smelling the delicious bakery smells from our shop downstairs.

"Hi, Mom."

"Oh, hi, Felicia." My mom sounded sleepy but happy to hear from me, too. "How are you, honey? Is something wrong?"

"Oh . . . well . . . not really, I guess." I shifted the phone to my shoulder and started picking at a thread on my quilt. "My friends are sort of fighting again. It feels really weird."

"It's always hard when your friends aren't getting along, honey, but I'm sure it'll blow over. In a few days, you won't even remember what you were fighting about." I could hear my mom clicking off a light—probably the light in the living room. "Did you have a nice dinner?"

Dinner? I frowned. Did Mom know about our dinner at Penny's? Why else would she be asking? "Uh . . ."

"Your father told me that you were going to have dinner with a friend of his," Mom went on. "He called this morning to ask me to pick you up from school Friday. Did you have a good time?"

I couldn't believe this. Mom knew about Penny, and she wasn't even upset? How was that possible? "Uh . . . yeah. I mean, the food was kind of weird. And . . ."

"And what, honey?"

I paused, trying to think of what I wanted to say. It had all seemed much clearer before I picked up the phone. But then, the Mom in my head didn't like the idea of Penny, either. "It was . . . it just made me miss you."

My mom was quiet for a second. I could almost hear her thinking. It made me wonder what she was thinking about. "I miss you, too, Felicia," she said eventually. "But I'll see you Friday. And you know you can always call me if you get lonesome."

"I know."

"Okay, honey. I'm glad you had a good dinner. Now I'd better get to bed, or I'll be falling asleep in the frosting tomorrow!"

I laughed in spite of myself. I could just see my mom, facedown in a bowl of chocolate frosting. It's hard work running a bakery.

"Okay, Mom. I love you. Good night."

"I love you, too, Felicia. Sleep tight." I heard the phone click softly.

I sat on my bed for a minute, then put the phone down and stood up. I walked over to my computer and clicked on the e-mail icon. Maybe writing to Arielle would make me feel better. I started a new message and typed in Arielle's address.

Hey Arielle,

    Horrible night! Went to dinner with my dad at Penny's. She's soooo weird! You should see her house.

    I hope she and my dad don't start dating. I don't know what I would do.

Love,
Felicia

*I don't know what I would do*, I read, clicking on the "send" icon. I really didn't. I couldn't imagine having Penny around all the time. It was hard enough just being around her for one night. What would it be like having Penny for a *mom?* Ooooh! I shuddered and pushed the thought from my mind. It was too scary to think about.

I closed the e-mail window and looked at the blank screen for a minute, thinking about the strange night. I had thought that calling Mom would make me feel better. Instead, I was more confused than ever.

# chapter
## SEVEN

**List posted on the orchestra room bulletin board:**

WLMS Orchestra DOs and DON'Ts
1. DO practice your scales, even if they're boring.
2. DON'T be afraid to ask for help if you're having trouble.
3. DO take good care of your instrument and keep it clean.
4. DON'T empty your spit valve on your neighbor.
5. DO remember to play your best and have fun!

"So what happened last night?"

I glanced up from my locker. Arielle was standing behind me. I guess she got my e-mail. As usual, Arielle looked great. How did she manage to keep every auburn hair on her head looking sleek and perfect all the time? My black curls ran wild no matter what I did to try to tame them.

But I was glad to see her, perfect hair and all. "Hi," I said gratefully. "It was pretty awful."

Arielle leaned against the next locker. "Your e-mail

97

didn't say much," she went on. "Did you really go to Penny's house for dinner last night?"

I nodded. "Didn't Amanda tell you about it on the bus?"

"My mom dropped me off this morning," Arielle said. "I haven't even seen Amanda yet. Why? What happened?"

I quickly filled her in on all the highlights. Or maybe that should be *low*lights. I left out the part about calling my mom, though. I wasn't sure how I felt about that.

"Wow," Arielle said when I'd finished. "That's harsh. I can't believe your dad still likes Penny."

"Tell me about it." I shut my locker door. It was almost time for the first bell. "It's not like they have anything in common."

We walked down the hall. I was feeling a little better. It was nice to have someone to talk to—someone who understood. A true friend.

There was a shriek of laughter from somewhere ahead. It sounded like Traci. The hall was crowded, so it took me a second to spot her. Traci was leaning against the water fountain near her locker. Ryan Bradley was standing in front of her, jumping around with a goofy look on his face.

Arielle spotted them, too. "What *is* he doing?" she asked.

I glanced at her sideways, trying to see whether she

looked impressed. "I think he's pretending to be a dog," I guessed as Ryan started crawling around on the floor, panting and barking at Traci's feet.

Arielle rolled her eyes. "Talk about puppy love," she quipped with a grin.

"Huh?" I blinked at her, wondering if I was missing something. Was she talking about herself or Traci. "What do you mean?"

"Don't tell me you haven't noticed!" Arielle exclaimed. "Traci and Ryan are totally crushing on one another."

"No way," I said uncertainly, glancing over at Traci and Ryan again. They hadn't noticed us—Traci was shoving Ryan away as he panted in her face.

"Way," Arielle replied firmly. "She always gets all giggly and stupid when his name comes up. And it comes up a *lot*."

I stopped to think. Now that she mentioned it, I realized that Ryan's name *had* been coming up a lot lately. I'd thought it was because *Arielle* liked him. But every time we talked about him, Traci had been present as well. Could it really be that *Traci* had a crush on him?

"Wow," I said slowly. "Are you sure?"

"Definitely," Arielle said confidently. "That's why she talks about him so much, and it's also why he stops by our table every single day at lunch."

Traci and Ryan. Could it be true? It *had* to be. Suddenly, it all made so much sense.

Just then, Traci glanced over and spotted us. Her smile faded, and she turned and hurried off in the opposite direction.

I gulped. For a second, I'd almost forgotten about all my problems. But now they came crashing down on me once again. What difference did it make who Traci liked or didn't like if she wasn't even talking to me?

As soon as I walked into the cafeteria a little later that day, I knew it was going to be bad news. Traci and Amanda were already sitting at our usual table. I clutched my lunch bag tightly. What was I supposed to do now? After everything that had happened, I couldn't just go over there and sit down with them as if everything was normal. Traci and Amanda might have the guts, but I didn't. Not even close.

Looking around for Arielle, I spotted her coming out of the lunch line. She was talking with some guy from our English class. I waved at her, but she didn't see me.

I hesitated, waiting for her to look around for me. Instead she hurried over and sat down with Traci and Amanda.

My heart sank. I guess I couldn't expect Arielle to ditch her other friends just for me. *She* wasn't the one that they were mad at. I was out of the group. I might as well get used to it.

Suddenly feeling like a complete idiot standing

there by myself, I quickly sat down at the nearest empty table. It felt kind of weird. We'd all been sitting together at the other table—*our* table—since the first day of school. And now here I was, all alone again. I felt miserable.

I looked over at the others. Amanda was saying something to Traci, who let out a snort of laughter. Arielle laughed, too.

My cheeks turned pink. Were they talking about me?

I closed my eyes. I didn't know what to do.

"Hi, there, Felicia," a new voice said. "Is anyone sitting here?"

I opened my eyes. A tall, skinny kid with big ears was standing in front of me. I recognized him from my math class, although I couldn't remember his name. Kurt? Kent? Something like that.

"Um, no," I said, even though I really wanted to be alone. If I couldn't be with my best friends, I didn't really want to talk to anyone.

"Thanks." Kurt-Kent plopped himself into the seat across from me and opened his lunch bag. "So why are you sitting over here, anyway?" he asked, his voice embarrassingly loud. "I thought you usually sat over by the windows with Arielle and her friends."

"Yeah," I said shortly. "But I'm sitting here today."

"Oh, okay." After that, Kurt-Kent started blabbing about our latest math quiz.

But I wasn't really listening. As I forced down my lunch, I kept sneaking looks over at Amanda, Traci, and Arielle. All I could think about was how much I wished all four of us were sitting together. Talking and laughing, just like we used to.

". . . Felicia? Earth to Felicia!"

With a start, I realized that Arielle was standing at the end of the table, staring down at me. "Hey!" I blurted, so surprised to see her that I almost choked on the bite of sandwich I was chewing. "I mean, hi!"

"What are you doing over here sitting with Karl?" Arielle asked.

Karl. So *that* was his name. He looked up at Arielle and smiled. "What did *you* think of that math quiz yesterday? I know I got an A. It was so easy!"

Arielle just shook her head in disbelief and turned back at me. "Felicia?"

"Um . . ." I wasn't sure what to say. Didn't Arielle realize that I wasn't like her? I couldn't just walk up to people who were mad at me and sit down with them like nothing had happened?

Arielle didn't wait for me to come up with a better answer. Checking her watch, she gestured toward the door. "Come on," she said. "Let's get out of here. I'll walk you to class. See you, Karl."

"Bye!"

"Okay," I said gratefully. "Bye, Karl." I stood up. Suddenly, everything looked the tiniest bit brighter.

At least I had one friend left. And one was definitely way better than none.

"Yo, Fiol!"

I glanced up from trying to dig my flute case out of the bottom of my locker. Ryan Bradley was grinning down at me, holding his violin case on one shoulder like a lumberjack with an ax.

"Hi," I muttered. Seeing him reminded me of one thing—Traci. After what had happened at lunch, I was really nervous about seeing her in orchestra practice.

Ryan leaned against the next locker, cradling his violin like a baby. "So how about that new piece, huh?" he commented. "It's pretty tough. Think you're going to be able to get it today in rehearsal?"

"Of course," I snapped. "Unlike *some* people, *I* actually practice instead of goofing off."

Ryan's eyebrows shot up in surprise. "Oo-kay," he said, backing off. "Just asking."

I slumped against my locker as he hurried away. Why had I snapped at him like that? It wasn't even fair. Ryan had to practice to play as well as he did. He might be a goofball, but it wasn't his fault I was in a bad mood. This stupid fight was really getting to me.

Grabbing my flute, I stomped down the hall toward the orchestra room. I glanced at Traci as I entered, but she didn't look up. I wondered how she was doing on this piece. Before I went to bed last night, I had run through it a couple of times. I felt a little bit more confident, but it was still more difficult than any piece I'd played before.

I sighed and headed for my seat. Ryan came in right behind me and immediately started acting up, playing silly songs on his violin and cracking jokes. Most of the other orchestra members ignored him as they warmed up. But I just sat there, holding my flute and glaring at him. I wasn't in the mood for Ryan's weird sense of humor.

Then I noticed another person who definitely wasn't ignoring Ryan. Traci. Her clarinet was lying on her lap, and she giggled as Ryan started singing some goofy song.

My mind flashed back to what Arielle had said. It looked like Traci really *did* like Ryan. I didn't understand it. But then again, I didn't understand a lot of things Traci did lately. Like deciding she was better friends with Amanda than she was with me, for instance.

Just then, Traci glanced in my direction. I guess I was sort of staring at her. I tried to look friendly; maybe we could start talking about the piece. But she turned away quickly and started fiddling with her reed and her sheet music.

I slumped into my seat, feeling grouchier than ever.

"Okay, people!" Ms. McClintic strode into the room at that moment, trailing sheet music behind her. She's nice and a really good teacher, but she can be a little scatterbrained sometimes. "Listen up! I have a few comments before we get started."

The room quieted down. Even Ryan shut up and sat down with the other violinists.

Ms. McClintic smiled. "Thank you. Now, quite a few of you have come to me over the past day or two to complain about the new piece being too hard."

There were a few whispers and murmurs. I clutched my flute hopefully. I felt okay about playing it, but I knew a lot of kids in the room were worried.

"That's why today, I'm going to divide you into smaller groups," she told us. "That way we can practice it more intensely, with the others in your group giving you feedback. I'll go around to each group one at a time and help out. How does that sound?"

"Terrible," the kid behind me whispered.

Ms. McClintic didn't hear. She started reading out the names in each group. She listed several groups of four, then finally got to my name.

"Group four—Felicia Fiol on flute," she said, glancing at me with a smile. Then she checked her paper again. "Judd Phillips on trombone. Ryan Bradley on violin. And Traci McClintic on clarinet."

I froze. Talk about bad luck! Then again, maybe Ms. McClintic didn't know that Traci and I weren't friends anymore. Maybe she thought she was being nice by putting us together.

By the time I dragged myself over to my group, the rest of the quartet was already seated in a square. I took the empty chair facing Judd, trying not to look at Traci.

Ryan was goofing off again. Of course. He cleared his throat, pretended to straighten a nonexistent tie, and fiddled with his sheet music.

I guess he was pretending to be some famous musician getting ready for a big solo or something. It was pretty lame, even for him. But Traci giggled. Of course.

A lot of the other groups were already playing, but Ryan just kept acting silly. He grabbed Traci's clarinet and turned it upside down, holding it up to his face like a microphone.

"Testing, testing," he said in a falsetto voice.

Traci giggled again. "Give me that," she said, grabbing the clarinet back.

Finally, Judd blinked at the two of them from behind his thick glasses. "Um," he said in his high-pitched, nerdy voice. "Are we going to practice or what?"

"What," Ryan joked. But he handed back Traci's clarinet and picked up his violin. "Okay, okay," he said. "Let's play already."

"Well!" Ms. McClintic's voice interrupted brightly. "How are things going over here, group four?"

"Excellent," Ryan said.

We all stared up at the teacher for a long, silent moment. Judd cleared his throat and seemed about to say something.

"Um, we're ready," Traci spoke up quickly. "Come on, guys. Let's play it for her."

I gulped. How were we supposed to play as a group when we hadn't practiced a single note? We hadn't even warmed up. Still, if the others were going to fake it, I didn't want to be the one to give us away and get everyone in trouble. It would only make Traci hate me even more.

Ms. McClintic counted off for us, then we played. If you can call it that.

Ryan sounded pretty good, as usual. His violin wasn't exactly in tune, but he didn't embarrass himself.

Neither did I, at least not too much. I guess all my practicing must have paid off. It wasn't perfect, but I got through it somehow.

Judd and Traci didn't do as well. Judd kept falling behind and needing to stop and start again when we got to the next section. As for Traci—well, after about the third loud *squawk*, Ms. McClintic groaned and signaled for us all to stop.

"Nicely done, you two," she said to Ryan and me.

"Ryan, you might want to double-check your tuning. And, Felicia, maybe back off a touch on that middle section—it's supposed to be light and airy and pianissimo. But otherwise, very good job."

She turned to Judd next. He looked dejected. "Sorry, Ms. McClintic," he said. "I practiced and practiced, but I'm just not getting it."

"It's okay, Judd," Ms. McClintic said kindly. "Here's what I suggest . . ."

She went on, soothingly talking Judd through the piece. But I wasn't really listening. I was too busy wondering what Traci was thinking. She was staring down into her lap, looking miserable. Why was she playing so badly? Was she as upset about our whole stupid fight as I was? Or didn't she care if we stayed friends?

Finally, Ms. McClintic turned to Traci. "All right," she said sternly. "I know you can do better than that, Traci. You need to focus—and practice more."

"I *did* practice," Traci muttered, her cheeks bright pink. She shot Ryan a sidelong glance, looking embarrassed.

My eyes widened as I suddenly realized what was going on. Of course! Traci was playing badly because she was sitting right across from Ryan—the guy she liked. Every time she looked at her sheet music, she was practically staring right at him. And now, to make things even worse, she was getting yelled at right in front of him—by her own mother, no less. I felt a rush of sympathy for her, even though she was mad at me. I didn't understand what she saw in Ryan, but still, that was a lousy situation to be in.

Ms. McClintic sighed. Then she looked around at all four of us.

"All right," she said. "Let's take it again from the top."

"Wait," I blurted.

"Yes, Felicia?" Ms. McClintic looked at me expectantly.

I could feel my cheeks growing hot. Still, I plowed on. "Um, I was just wondering," I mumbled. "Uh, would it be okay if I switched seats with Ryan? I—I—" I glanced around desperately for an excuse. "Um, I can't concentrate when I'm facing the windows like this."

The other three members of the group looked at me like I was crazy. Ms. McClintic raised one eyebrow.

"All right, Felicia," she said. "If Ryan has no objection, I suppose it would be all right."

Ryan shrugged. "No problem."

Feeling kind of stupid, I stood and gathered up my music. Soon I was sitting across from Traci instead of Ryan. I didn't know if it would help or not or if Traci even knew what I was up to. But I couldn't just sit there and watch her struggling without trying to do something about it.

She was still my friend even if I wasn't hers anymore.

# chapter
## EIGHT

**New WLMS Cafeteria Rules:**

ALL STUDENTS PLEASE READ!

1. Stay seated at your table unless you're going to the lunch line, trash cans, or rest rooms.
2. Obey all teachers' instructions.
3. Throwing food or causing other trouble in the cafeteria will result in detention for a minimum of TWO WEEKS.

"All right, people!" Ms. McClintic clapped. "That was much better! You'll all be ready for the fall concert in no time."

"Ugh!" I groaned along with everyone else. It was true that our last time through the piece had definitely been an improvement over the first few times. But that really wasn't saying much.

Ms. McClintic laughed. "Okay, class dismissed. Now get out of here, and I'll see you next time. Don't forget to practice!"

It took me a few minutes to pack up my flute and

sheet music. By the time I stood up and looked around the orchestra room, Traci was nowhere in sight.

When I headed out into the hallway, I spotted her right away. Traci was standing a little way down the hall, her back to me. Her backpack was lying on the floor nearby, and she was still holding her clarinet.

I paused, watching her. She ripped the reed off her clarinet's mouthpiece and flung it at the trash can by the wall.

It missed, bouncing off the rim and landing on the floor. With a loud groan, Traci leaned over and snatched it up, flicking it toward the can again.

Once again, it missed. I couldn't help wincing as a couple of eighth-grade boys walking by laughed.

"Nice shot, hotshot," one of the boys joked.

Traci scowled at them and bent to pick up the reed again. This time she marched up to the trash can and dropped it in. When she turned around to pick up her stuff, I could see that she was near tears. I couldn't believe she was so upset. Was it our fight or the difficult piece?

Well, either way, I had to talk to her. Even if she hated me.

"Hey," I said, walking up to her. "Don't worry. You weren't the only one who was having trouble today. Besides, you sounded really good the last few times."

Traci stared at me in surprise. For a second, she looked suspicious.

Then she sighed. "Thanks," she muttered. "But I wish my mom would just let me quit. I stink. This piece just proves it."

"No way," I countered. "You're really good. Your mom knows it, too—otherwise she wouldn't get on your case like that. She'd just pat you on the head like she does with Judd and give up."

I could tell she was thinking about that. Finally, she shrugged. "Maybe," she admitted. "But I'd better do some serious practicing before next rehearsal. I definitely don't want to get humiliated like that again in this lifetime."

I nodded. Personally, I suspected that Ryan's presence had more to do with it than a lack of practice. Otherwise Traci's playing wouldn't have improved so much as soon as I'd switched seats with Ryan.

I didn't say anything, though. "Maybe we could practice together," I suggested tentatively. "You could come over to my mom's place this weekend. She's a pretty good coach, and she could accompany us on the piano."

Traci smiled a little. "Okay." She paused. "So . . . does this mean we're okay or what?"

I was so relieved that I almost dropped my flute. "I hope so," I said, smiling gratefully.

113

Traci took a step toward me. "Look," she said. "I think I understand why you've been so upset the past couple of days. Well, sort of."

"What do you mean?" I asked cautiously.

"I was thinking about it in orchestra just now," Traci said. "I guess I wasn't listening to your side of things. But I also think you weren't listening to Amanda's."

Oh, no. I couldn't believe my ears. She was doing it again—taking Amanda's side. But she looked so earnest that I decided to hear her out.

"Yes?" I prompted.

Traci started taking her clarinet apart as she talked. "You're upset because you don't like Penny much and you don't want her dating your dad. Right?"

"Pretty much," I said.

"Well, Amanda is upset because she *does* like Penny and you're going around slamming her when you haven't really given her a chance." Traci glanced at me as she tucked her mouthpiece into its slot in her clarinet case. "I know you don't really mean to come across that way," she added hastily. "But still—can't you see how it makes Amanda feel when you make fun of Penny or talk about how you don't want her dating your dad?"

I thought about it. How would I feel if someone was bad-mouthing one of my friends? I'd never really considered it that way before.

"I guess," I said slowly. "But I didn't like it when Amanda started saying my dad wasn't cool enough for Penny, either. And I know what you're going to say—she didn't mean it that way." I shrugged. "But that's how it sounded."

"I know," Traci said, shutting her clarinet case and picking it up. "But if you talked to her about it, I bet she'd apologize. Just like you'd apologize to her. Right?"

"I guess."

"By the way," Traci added softly, "I'm sorry, too. I should have talked to you sooner. I guess I just took Amanda's side because I like Penny so much, too. She really is pretty cool when you give her a chance."

I just nodded. I doubted I would ever agree with her opinion of Penny, but I wanted to be nice. Because I really, really, really hated fighting with my friends.

I reached out and touched Traci's arm. "I am sorry," I said. "I never wanted to fight with you."

Traci smiled. Then she reached over and hugged me.

"Good," she said. "So now that *we're* officially made up, we're halfway back to normal already!"

I smiled back at her. Traci has always been a glass-half-full kind of person. It was one of the things I liked best about her. "Cool," I said.

"So should I talk to Amanda about this tonight and

see if we can get things completely back to normal?" Traci asked.

"Definitely," I agreed, feeling happier already. "And I'll call Arielle."

The first chance we all got to talk was the next day at lunch.

I sat down across from Amanda. "So . . . ," I began uncertainly.

Then I fell silent. I wasn't sure what else to say, so I glanced over at Traci for help.

"Okay," Arielle said impatiently. "Felicia—Amanda. You both want to make up, so just go ahead and do it already."

Amanda took a deep breath. "You're right, Arielle," she said. "Felicia, I'm sorry. I didn't mean to say anything bad about your dad. I guess I was kind of insensitive."

"Me too," I blurted, relieved that she'd gone first. "I'm so sorry I made fun of Penny. And—and everything." I didn't bother to go into details. The last thing I wanted was to say the wrong thing again.

"Cool," Arielle put in, opening her lunch bag. "Does this mean we're all friends again?"

"Definitely," Amanda and I said at the same time. Then we both laughed.

"So," Amanda said, picking up her sandwich, "I

have my student government orientation meeting today. I'm really excited."

Arielle giggled. "I would be, too. That student government president, Asher Bank, is *hot*."

Traci smirked. "Yeah, Amanda," she said. "I'd join student government, too, just to get to stare at him awhile longer."

Amanda rolled her eyes. "Whatever, guys." She took a sip of her apple juice. "I joined student government because I want to get involved. They're talking about cutting the funding for our arts program! I really want to help prevent that."

Arielle frowned. "Why do they want to do that, anyway?"

"They want to spend more money on the sports teams." Amanda shrugged. "It's silly, really."

"Hey . . ." Arielle brightened. "I wonder if they'd spend more money on the soccer team. Like, new uniforms!"

"Yeah!" Traci grinned. "If we get to the state championships this year, we want to look really good."

"Come on, guys." Amanda gave Traci and Arielle a serious look. "Would you want to lose art class for new uniforms? We should have the chance to have both arts programs *and* sports."

"I guess." Arielle gazed lazily at her peach fingernails.

I could see Amanda was starting to get upset, so I reached out and put my hand on her arm. "I think you're right, Amanda," I said. "I'm glad you're going to do something about it."

Amanda looked surprised, but then she smiled a warm smile. "Thanks, Felicia." She grinned mischievously. "You're such a creative type, I knew you'd understand."

I laughed, thinking of Penny and that weird dinner party. I was so glad to be Amanda's friend again.

Just then our English teacher, Mrs. Scott, stopped by our table. "Everything okay over here, girls?"

At first I wasn't sure what she was talking about. Then I realized she was on food-fight patrol. There were at least six teachers wandering around the cafeteria during sixth-grade lunch that day instead of the normal two or three.

I smiled at Amanda as I answered. "Absolutely, Mrs. Scott," I said. "Everything is great here."

The teacher moved on. Suddenly, Arielle leaned forward and looked at Amanda.

"Hey! Maybe I can meet you after your student government thing today and you can introduce me to Asher?"

Amanda looked sort of annoyed. "Arielle, I'm serious about student government and trying to make a difference. I don't even *know* Asher yet."

"Oh, but you'll get to know him." Arielle grinned wickedly. "Unless you're planning to keep him all for yourself?"

Amanda looked up at Arielle. I could tell that she didn't think Arielle's question was funny at all. In fact, that angry little line was forming between her eyebrows. I panicked—the last thing I wanted was for the four of us to end up in a fight again. I had to change the subject, *fast!*

"Hey, about Penny," I broke in. "I guess we're all on the same side again. Now what do we do?"

"Do about what?" Amanda asked, reaching for one of her carrot sticks.

Arielle shrugged. "Face it—as long as Penny and Mr. Fiol are still seeing each other, you guys are going to feel weird, right?"

"Right, but so what?" Amanda stirred her yogurt. "What are we supposed to do about that? They're adults—they like each other, they can do whatever they want."

"True," Arielle said. "But their relationship is what messed up our whole friendship in the first place. And it's not like any of us think the two of them belong together."

"You know, she's right," I said thoughtfully. "It would be a lot easier to forget about all of this if Dad and Penny just went their separate ways." I chose my words carefully, trying not to say anything that Amanda could take wrong.

"True," Amanda agreed. "Um, not that there's anything wrong with either one of them, of course. But they really don't seem right for each other."

119

I smiled at her. She was trying, too.

Traci shrugged and popped a potato chip into her mouth. "They'll probably realize that soon enough themselves, right?"

"Sure," Arielle said, raising one eyebrow. "So why not help them along? That would make it easier on everyone. Especially us. Do we want to go through another week like this one?"

Traci shuddered. "No way," she said. "But what can we do? Like Amanda said, they're adults. They're not going to stop seeing each other just because we don't like it."

"Not unless we can come up with some kind of plan . . . ," I began thoughtfully.

Just then Ryan came bounding up to the table. "Hey," he greeted us. "You're all sitting together. Does that mean you're friends again?"

Traci rolled her eyes. "For your information, we were always friends," she told him. "We were just having a—um—slight disagreement."

"Ri-i-ight," Ryan said with a grin. "Sort of like World War Two?"

I glanced at Arielle, who winked. It was obvious to both of us that Ryan was really there to talk to Traci. It would have been kind of entertaining, except I wasn't in the mood. I wanted to get back to our conversation. Could we really come up with a way to break up Dad and Penny?

Ryan was still blabbing—something about Lola and a cooling meat loaf. I spaced out, trying to come up with a good plan.

I snapped back to reality when Traci poked me on the shoulder. "I've got it!" she hissed.

"What?" I asked, a little distracted.

She leaned closer and started whispering. My eyes widened as I heard her plan. It was sneaky. It was devious.

Most important, it just might work.

# chapter
## NINE

**Notes passed in English class, Thursday after lunch:**

Hey, Amanda,
    Did you call her yet? What did she say?
                                    F. F.

F.—
    I CALLED HER FROM THE OFFICE RIGHT
AFTER LUNCH. SHE'S IN!
                    AMANDA

Traci,
    Amanda called her. We're all set.
    Keep your fingers crossed—this had better work!
                                    F. F.

Dear Felicia,
    Don't worry! It'll work. It HAS TO!!!!!!
                                    Traci

Yo, Felicia—
    You'd better stop passing notes, girlie. I just saw

Mrs. S. give you a dirty look! Ha! And you def.
DON'T want to get detention today!
Arielle

"Can I feed the ferrets?" Amanda asked.

"Sure," I replied. "Their food is in the green-and-white bag in the last metal can outside."

A funny-looking little sheltie mix barked at me hungrily. I poured the rest of the food from my scoop into her dish, then glanced around, deciding what to do next. Traci was cleaning out one of the dog runs. Amanda was just hurrying back in from getting the ferret food. Even Arielle was helping—she giggled as a flop-eared rabbit nibbled lettuce out of her hand.

I smiled, pushing my curly hair back off my forehead. This was more like it. I couldn't believe how great it felt to be hanging out with all three of my best friends again. Working together.

I checked my watch. Arielle saw me. "Relax, Felicia," she said. "It's not time yet. She'll be here."

"I just hope this plan works," Amanda commented, sounding worried. "Are you sure there's not another way?"

"Not one that's definitely going to work," I replied firmly. I didn't want her to back out now.

Traci nodded. "I know it seems a little mean," she told Amanda. "But it'll work out the best for everyone in the long run."

"I guess," Amanda said, though she still didn't sound convinced.

I grabbed a couple of water dishes out of the nearest runs. Hurrying outside, I dumped the bowls in the grass and then refilled them at the pump.

As I picked up the full dishes, I noticed that my hands were shaking. Amanda wasn't the only one who was nervous about this plan. But I definitely wasn't going to back out now. Not when we were so close.

I hurried back into the shelter. Most of the dogs had finished eating, so it was getting pretty noisy in there.

"What else do we need to do?" Traci shouted as I entered.

I set the water bowls carefully back into the pens before answering. "Nothing," I replied, brushing off my hands on my jeans as I turned to face Traci. "I think we're done."

Amanda nodded, glancing around. "Everybody's been fed," she said over the barking. "Should we go outside where it's a little quieter?"

"Sure," I agreed.

As we passed Quentin's run, he jumped up against the wire, barking loudly. "Sorry, little buddy," I told him, pausing just long enough to scratch his ears through the cage. "We can't take you outside right now."

The four of us headed for the grassy area

between the shelter and the driveway, where we could see if anyone drove up. We sat there for a few minutes, picking at the grass and talking about nothing much. It was so obvious how nervous we all were.

Finally, Traci checked her watch and sighed. "What time did you tell Penny to pick you up?" she asked Amanda. "If she doesn't get here soon, Ryan will beat her here."

Arielle shot me a brief smirk, then turned to Traci. "Don't worry," she told her. "If Ryan gets here early, I'm sure *you* can figure out a way to distract him for a few minutes."

I stifled a giggle. Traci frowned at her in confusion. Before she could answer, we all heard the sound of a motor. Penny's car was pulling into the driveway.

"Okay," Amanda said nervously, jumping to her feet. "Here goes nothing."

"Yeah," I muttered. "Ryan better get here soon."

We all walked over to the driveway to meet Penny as she parked the car. She climbed out and waved to us. She was wearing a long, flowy skirt with funky patterns embroidered on it and a gauzy white blouse. Her blond hair was pulled back with sparkly clips. I had to admit it—she looked pretty.

"Hi, girls," she called cheerfully. "How are you all doing?"

"Fine," we chorused.

Amanda stepped forward. "Can you hang out for a second?" she invited. "I need to get my stuff out of the kennel."

"Sure," Penny said.

Traci stepped forward. "Hey, want a tour of the shelter?" she asked brightly. "You haven't seen it yet, have you?"

"Oh." The sunny smile left Penny's face immediately. She gulped as she glanced toward the backyard. The sound of dogs barking was still audible, even where we were standing. "Um, I don't know. . . ."

"Come on, it'll be fun," Arielle said in her most convincing voice. "Don't you want to see what Mr. F. does all day?"

Amanda smiled at Penny. "Don't worry, all the dogs are kenneled," she said. "We'll just take a quick peek. There are some really cute rabbits in the shelter right now. Didn't you tell me once that you had a pet bunny when you were our age?"

"Yes," Penny said, a slight smile returning to her face. "His name was Puff." She took a deep breath. "Okay," she said. "Lead the way, girls. I guess it is time I checked out the shelter Luis is always talking about."

I smiled gratefully at my friends as we headed for the backyard. We made quite a team.

"So, Felicia, is your dad around?" Penny asked as we walked.

I almost rolled my eyes. But I answered politely. "No, he's not home right now," I said. "He has lots of meetings to go to."

"Oh." Penny didn't say anything else for a second. When we reached the shelter entrance, the noise was deafening. She smiled nervously. "Boy, they sure are loud."

"That's dogs for you," Traci said with a shrug. "You get used to it after a while. Especially if you live with it full-time, like Felicia and her dad do."

As Penny peered into the shelter, I flashed Traci a thumbs-up.

Amanda led the way inside. Penny followed, though she stayed well away from the dog runs. Several of the dogs flung themselves at the gates to their pens, making Penny jump a little.

"That's Dad's favorite right there," I said, pointing out a huge mixed breed that looked a little like a wolf. He was as sweet a dog as could be, but even I could see that he was pretty scary-looking. "He's thinking about adopting him himself."

That was a total lie, but Penny bought it. Her eyes widened, and I saw her gulp. "He's—cute," she said weakly. "What's his name?"

"Killer," I said quickly. I could hear Arielle stifling a laugh. Actually, the dog's name was Herbert, but *Killer* sounded so much more frightening.

Penny nodded shakily. "Hello . . . Killer." She tried to smile, but she moved as far from Herbert's cage as possible. Herbert looked a little confused. I reached in and gave him a quick pat.

We continued to introduce her to various dogs. Penny was trying, I had to give her that. She smiled bravely the whole time and even managed to say something nice about most of the dogs. But her face was pale, and she was practically shaking.

"What do you think?" Traci asked when we reached the end of the dog section.

"They're great," Penny replied with a nervous laugh. "I guess I'll have to get used to being around dogs if I want to spend time with Luis." She took a step toward the last pen in the row. A tiny Chihuahua mix was inside, curled against the wire pen, blinking at us sleepily. "Maybe I can start with the little ones—like this one." She stuck her fingers through the wire and briefly tickled the little dog behind the ears. He wagged his tail happily, and she giggled.

I grimaced. Penny obviously wasn't getting the hint. Luckily, we had other things in store for her.

After a brief visit to the rabbit cages, we all headed back outside. I sneaked a peek at my watch. Where was Ryan? He was supposed to be here already.

As I stepped out into the afternoon sunshine, a deep, loud, happy bark answered my question. A huge mass of brown-and-white fur came bounding up to us, barking and panting and drooling happily, the leash hanging loose from her collar.

"Lola!" a desperate voice shouted from the driveway. A second later, Ryan raced into view, panting and looking worried.

Meanwhile, Lola was greeting all of us the way she liked best—by leaping up, planting her enormous front paws on our chests, and enthusiastically placing a slobbery kiss on our faces.

Traci was first. Then Amanda.

Then Lola threw herself on Penny.

I guess Penny was so startled at first that she didn't say anything. Then as Lola started trying to lick her face, she let out an ear-piercing shriek. Shoving Lola away, she turned and raced for the driveway, still screaming.

Confused, Lola went bounding after Penny, barking enthusiastically.

Ryan looked even more confused, too. I felt kind of bad for him. As far as he knew, he and Lola were just supposed to show up for another training session with Dad. The plan was working, though; there was no time for explanation.

I took off after Lola with my friends right behind me.

# chapter
## TEN

**Instant messages:**

```
sockrgrl0: Hey, girlz, every1 still alive?
PrincessA: Barely. My 'rents r still steamin.
   FiFio1: So what r we going 2 do??
FlowerGrl: I don't know. A wk is a long time. :(
sockrgrl0: Oops. Mom is calling me. CU all 2mor-
           row in school. . . .
```

By the time my friends and I got to the driveway,
Penny was in her car. She was sitting in the driver's
seat, shaking and crying as Lola flung herself happily against the window, slobbering all over the
glass.

Ryan skidded up behind us. "What's going on?" he
demanded breathlessly. "Who is that?"

He sounded pretty worried. Without waiting for an
answer, he ran over and grabbed Lola by the collar,
dragging her away from Penny's car.

"Lola, *sit*!" Ryan shouted.

Lola looked perplexed, but she obediently lowered

her rump to the ground, staring up at her owner expectantly.

Ryan picked up Lola's leash, which was still trailing from her collar. After a quick, anxious glance at Penny, whose face was buried in her hands, Ryan hurried back over to us with Lola trotting along beside him.

"Who is that?" he asked again.

"Penny, my baby-sitter," Amanda spoke up, her voice a little shaky. "Um, she's really afraid of dogs."

Ryan shook his head and glanced at Traci with a frown. "Did you know she would be here?" he asked. "Why did you tell me to let Lola off the leash as soon as I got here? I thought Mr. Fiol wanted to test her jumping-up-on-people thing. Where is he, anyway?"

Traci gulped and avoided his eyes. "Um . . . ," she began.

I felt my face flame. Ryan sounded really mad at Traci, which made me feel terrible. Telling him to let Lola off her leash had been *my* idea.

"Never mind," Ryan said. He scowled at Traci before she could answer and tossed her Lola's leash. "Here, hold her for a minute."

Then he turned and hurried back toward Penny's car. The four of us watched him.

"Looks like the plan worked," Arielle breathed.

I glanced over at the car. Ryan was tapping gently on the window. We could hear him calling to Penny, his voice soothing.

"I'm really sorry," he said. "Lola's just a puppy—she didn't mean any harm. She just has a lot of energy—too much sometimes. But I'm sorry she scared you."

Penny gazed at him blankly, tears still streaming down her face. She didn't answer.

"You can come out now," Ryan continued. His voice was really gentle—I'd never heard him sound like that before. "I'll lock Lola up in one of the empty kennels if you want. Then you'll be safe for sure."

Penny said something to him, but I couldn't hear it from where my friends and I were standing.

"I know," Ryan responded to her soothingly. "She's really big. I don't blame you for being startled. It's totally understandable."

Was this really the same goofy, loudmouthed kid I'd known for years? I couldn't believe Ryan sounded so caring and kind and concerned about someone he didn't even know. I guess I'd misjudged him. He was definitely more than just the class clown.

But there was no time to thank Ryan for being so considerate or apologize for not telling him what we were up to. My father's car was pulling into the driveway.

I gulped, realizing I was going to have plenty of apologies to make. Just as soon as Dad found out what we'd done . . .

I picked at a splinter on the edge of the kitchen chair as Dad hit the hang-up button on the phone. "Okay, Arielle," he said sternly. "You're next."

In a meek voice Arielle recited her phone number. Dad dialed it and waited. Arielle, Amanda, Traci, and I stared at one another from our seats around the table. Every one of them looked just as unhappy as I felt.

"Hello, Mrs. Davis?" he said when someone on the other end answered. "This is Luis Fiol, Felicia's father. I'm afraid our daughters got themselves in a bit of trouble this afternoon. . . ."

As Dad went on, telling the entire horrible story for the third time in a row, I shot a glance at Penny. She was sitting on the tall stool near the stove with a cup of tea on the counter in front of her. She looked a lot calmer now—in fact, she looked a whole lot calmer than my father did at the moment. I wondered if she would ever be able to forgive us.

". . . and so that's why I think the girls shouldn't be allowed to see each other outside of school for a week," Dad said. "A little time apart to think about all this will be good for them. Do I have your cooperation on that?" He listened for a second, then nodded. "Thank you. That's no problem. I'll swing by and drop off Arielle in a few minutes."

He said good-bye and hung up. Then he turned to face the four of us, rubbing his hands together.

"All right," he said briskly. "That's that. Penny will drive Amanda home, and I'll take Traci and Arielle."

We all nodded meekly without saying a word. There really wasn't anything more to say. We'd already explained the whole rotten thing. How we'd wanted to scare Penny away from my dad. How Amanda had made sure Penny would be the one to pick her up from my house that afternoon. How Traci had made sure Ryan would show up at around the same time as Penny with Lola off her leash. How we'd taken Penny to look at the dogs in the shelter so she'd be nice and nervous when Lola showed up. All four of us had apologized to Penny. We'd also apologized to Ryan. Dad was furious.

The sad part was, I couldn't really blame him. How had things gotten so out of control, anyway? The plan had seemed like a good idea at the time. But now it just seemed stupid. Stupid and mean.

Dad stood up and grabbed his keys out of the bowl on the counter where he kept them. Arielle, Amanda, and Traci stood up, too.

"Well, I guess this is it," Traci muttered, shooting a slightly nervous glance at my father.

"Uh-huh." Amanda shrugged. "See you guys in school, right?"

"Right," Arielle and I said at the same time.

I felt like my heart was breaking as I watched them leave. Slumping in my chair, I rested my head in my hands.

My friends and I were broken up again, and this time it really was all my fault. How was I ever going to fix this?

"Hi," I said breathlessly, rushing over to our lunch table and flopping down in the empty seat next to Traci. Amanda and Arielle were already sitting across the table. "Boy, am I glad to see you guys!"

"Where were you before homeroom?" Arielle asked, peeling back the lid on her yogurt.

I grimaced. "Dad made me clean out all the kennels before school," I said. "It took so long, I missed the bus, so he drove me."

"I have a bunch of extra chores for the next two weeks, too," Traci said. "I have to clean all the bathrooms and take out the trash and do the whole family's laundry—including Dave's stinky socks. Ugh! Talk about smelly!"

I felt terrible. "I'm sorry," I whispered. "It's all my fault we're in trouble now."

Amanda looked at me in surprise. "What do you mean?" she said. "It's not your fault. I mean, not *only* yours. We were all there."

"Yeah, but it was my fault we got into this mess in

the first place," I pointed out. "Because of my, um, problem with my dad and Penny."

Traci leaned over and hugged me. "Don't be ridiculous," she ordered. "Your problems are our problems. All for one and one for all."

That made me feel a tiny bit better. It was great to have such loyal friends. How could I ever have doubted them before? They knew I wasn't perfect, and they didn't care—they liked me, anyway.

*They're not going to write me off for one stupid mistake*, I thought. Not like I did with Penny . . .

I bit my lip as I thought back to my first meeting with Penny. Remembering it now, I couldn't believe I'd been so judgmental. What if my friends had been the same way? What if Arielle and Amanda had just gone on assuming I was some shy, boring person with nothing to say? They never would have seen the real me. Even Traci might have decided I wasn't worth the trouble anymore.

And that was exactly how I'd treated Penny . . .

"Oh!" Suddenly, I realized what we needed to do. "I've got it," I said. "I have a plan to fix everything!"

"A plan?" Amanda said cautiously. "Um, are you sure another plan is a good idea right now?"

Arielle shook her head. "No, Felicia's right," she declared. "We definitely need a plan. I mean, come on. We're already grounded. How much worse could it get?"

"I really think this could work," I said. "I was thinking about it earlier when I was cleaning out Quentin's pen."

Traci gasped. "Quentin!" she exclaimed. "That reminds me, what are we going to do about pet therapy? We're supposed to go back to the hospital this weekend, but if we aren't allowed to see each other—"

"Wait," I interrupted. "If my plan works, we might not even be grounded anymore by this weekend."

Amanda looked skeptical. "This had better be a really good plan, Felicia," she said. "My parents are pretty mad."

I took a deep breath. "It *is* a good plan," I said confidently. "See, I was thinking about pet therapy. And also about how Penny patted that tiny little dog at the shelter yesterday. Remember?"

Traci nodded. "She said something about wanting to get used to dogs so she could hang out with your father."

I winced. I wasn't totally crazy about the idea of Dad and Penny spending lots of time together. But I was even less crazy about being separated from my friends.

"Right," I said. "So what if we used some of the same methods we use for pet therapy—only we use them to help Penny get used to being around dogs?"

"I don't know," Arielle said doubtfully. "After the way Lola freaked her out yesterday, I doubt Penny will want anything to do with dogs for a long, long time."

138

Amanda looked thoughtful. "I'm not so sure about that. Yesterday on the way home, Penny said something about how she overreacted, and she knew Lola wasn't trying to hurt her. I think maybe Lola's slurp attack might actually have helped her realize she shouldn't be so afraid." She smiled wryly. "Sort of like shock therapy, I guess."

"Excellent!" I exclaimed. "Then all we need to do is expose her to some nice, gentle dogs. Maybe starting with some small, quiet ones, like that Chihuahua mix. Then when she's comfortable with those, we move on to bigger, more active ones, like Quentin. We could even invite her to come along to pet therapy with us so she can see how sweet the dogs are with the sick people at the hospital. Eventually, we can work our way up to bigger and bigger dogs. And before she knows it, Penny will be a total dog lover!"

"Wow." Arielle sounded impressed. "That really does sound like a good plan. And I bet our parents will let us try since we'll be trying to make up for what we did before. You know, taking responsibility and stuff."

"Yeah, my parents love talking about responsibility. They'll probably let us try," Traci agreed. She wrinkled her nose. "I'll probably still be stuck washing my stinky brother's stinky socks, though."

Amanda laughed and nodded. "I'm sure my parents will go along with it, too. They're crazy about Penny."

139

"But do you think Penny will go for it?" I asked worriedly.

"I think I could talk her into giving it a try," Amanda said. She smiled. "You know, Felicia, I think this just might work! You're brilliant!"

I smiled, feeling proud of myself. Okay, so maybe I'd messed up. Maybe I'd messed up a *lot*. But at least I was trying to fix it now. I was even sort of looking forward to it. It felt really good to help the people at the hospital with our pet therapy visits. It would definitely feel just as good to help Penny get over her fears.

Traci put her hand out across the table. "Are we all in?" she asked.

I nodded and put my hand over hers. Amanda put her hand on mine. Then Arielle added hers.

"All for one and one for all!" I cried, and we all raised our hands with a whoop.

I grinned, feeling a lot happier than I'd felt all week. This was my favorite part of my new plan. I was part of a group again.

And that was the best feeling of all.

**Don't Miss**

# wondergirls #4

## "And the Winner Is..."

**coming this fall!**

Class elections are rolling around, and with the school board deciding whether to cut arts funding at Wonder Lake Middle School, Amanda *really* wants to run for office to try to make a difference! With the help of Arielle, Traci, and Felicia, Amanda's sure that she will be elected president of her class. But the closer elections get, the less time Amanda is spending with her friends. And when someone else decides to help Amanda—a *cute* someone whom Arielle has a crush on—the trouble begins. Suddenly, Amanda's facing some very tough competition.

*Can the Wonder Girls pull together in time to help Amanda get elected?*